"Look, I have enough to handle with two kids and a business. I don't have time for a relationship or…whatever other kind of business you think we're going to do."

Danny's eyebrows almost disappeared into the curls on his forehead. "A relationship?"

"That's right."

"Who the hell said anything about a relationship?"

"You just propositioned me."

"The hell I did."

Tessa wasn't buying it. She crossed her arms and gave him her big-bad-mom stare. "Then what was all that bedroom stuff?"

Danny clenched his jaw, flushing to the roots of his hair, but whether it was embarrassment or anger, Tessa couldn't tell. "I don't need to proposition strangers to get them into bed. I need a babysitter."

Dear Reader,

A close friend who had gotten divorced inspired this novel. She had two children in tow, and plunged back into the dating world only to discover that most of the men she dated had children of their own also. For me, this led to tons of fun questions such as: What if we get serious and the kids hate each other? What if the kids love each other and the man and I don't get along? Then there is the babysitting problem—how can you ever see each other alone?

What better than to use the original situation's potential and write a story about Danny Santori, a fireman, who is a widower with four kids, and Tessa Doherty, a landscape designer, who is a divorcee with two kids. Danny and Tessa have lost their summer babysitters at the last minute. They're stuck until a friend comes up with the solution of putting them together.

The fun part of this was imagining all the antics of the children and their impact on the relationship. I called my local fire department and they rolled out the carpet so I could do the research. Plus, I got to hang around with firemen. What could be better than that?

Meg Lacey

The Fireman's Christmas

Meg Lacey

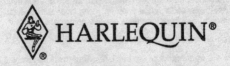

HARLEQUIN®

TORONTO • NEW YORK • LONDON
AMSTERDAM • PARIS • SYDNEY • HAMBURG
STOCKHOLM • ATHENS • TOKYO • MILAN • MADRID
PRAGUE • WARSAW • BUDAPEST • AUCKLAND

Recycling programs
for this product may
not exist in your area.

PLEASE RECYCLE • THIS PRODUCT IS RECYCLABLE

ISBN-13: 978-0-373-75285-0

THE FIREMAN'S CHRISTMAS

Copyright © 2009 by Lynn Miller.

www.eHarlequin.com

Printed in U.S.A.

ABOUT THE AUTHOR

Meg Lacey first discovered romance in the sixth grade when she wrote her own version of *Gone with the Wind*. However, her writing career didn't last. Instead she went into theater and studied acting and directing for her bachelor's and master's degrees and, finally, ended up in television as a writer-producer.

Over the years, she also dabbled in a few other areas. She has been an actress, director, copywriter, creative dramatics teacher, mime, mom, college instructor and a school bus driver (and wow, are there stories in that experience). She started two creative marketing and media companies in the Midwest and worked in all media from network cable programming to corporate initiatives, but through it all, she's always returned to writing. She has written for Silhouette Books as Lynn Miller and for the Harlequin Temptation line, and is now thrilled to join the Harlequin American Romance family.

She has three funny, mouthy, independent daughters who are now all married and creating chaos in someone else's life. She also has two little grandchildren and a wonderful husband. Guy is her true hero—he's survived life in a house with four women, two female cats and a female dog and can still remember how to tie his shoes. Without his marvelous sense of humor, patience and support, her life would be very different.

Visit Meg Lacey at www.meglacey.com.

Meg Lacey

To my friend Robin Graff-Reed
(aka Robin Wiete, Leanne Grayson)
for her continual support and inspiration.

To my husband, Guy, who keeps me sane
while I drive him insane; and to my daughters,
Jen, Sara and Jes, for the same reason.

To my agent, Karen Solem, who enthusiastically
welcomed me back from my writing hiatus.

Finally, to the men and women of the
Green Township Fire Department in Cincinnati, Ohio,
who were so generous with their time and knowledge.

Chapter One

Danny Santori looked up from the résumé in his hand. "Thank you for coming over on such short notice, Mrs...." His mind went blank. What was her name again? Staring at the austere woman seated in his cluttered front parlor, he felt a smile stretch his mouth until he was sure he resembled a grinning monkey. It was a hot day in Warenton, Pennsylvania, but the woman opposite him was dressed as if it was early spring with her long-sleeved buttoned-up blouse and gray cardigan.

God, he hated this! It was a royal pain, interviewing baby-sitters, explaining his situation over and over again. He hated the fact that his wife wasn't here to do it for him. Of course, if she had been, he wouldn't be in this predicament at all. Laurie had been perfectly content to be a full-time wife and mother, and had even given up her job when Danny suggested it due to his schedule. Danny realized he'd been a lucky man—now he was discovering how lucky. He stared blankly at the stern face before him. "Uh, Mrs...."

The older woman gave him the once-over with narrowed, suspicious eyes, then dropped her gaze to the frayed Oriental rug sprawled across the scarred hardwood floor.

Her mouth pursed as if she'd just sucked a lemon. "My name is Peach. P-E-A-C-H. *Miss.*"

Danny blinked, unable to reconcile the sweet name with this sour woman. He wished her stare didn't make him feel so much like an errant schoolboy. After all, he was supposed to be in charge here, wasn't he? He stood, hoping to feel more at ease once he was on his feet.

"I understand from the agency that you can be here day after tomorrow, Miss Peach. That's great, because my shift at the firehouse starts that day at 7:00 a.m. The kids probably won't be up at that time, which is why I was glad you could stop by today so I can introdu—oooofff!"

Danny staggered, then righted himself to look down at the small, round body that had just wrapped itself around his left leg. His almost-four-year-old daughter hung on as if she were resisting a hurricane wind. "Emma, let go, honey."

"Daddy," she demanded, hugging harder. "Walk me."

"Not now, Em. I'm talking to this nice lady."

Emma just held on, staring up at him with that heart-wrenching smile and tousled blond hair that reminded him so much of her mother. Danny's resistance sagged. "Okay, just once around."

With Emma clinging like Velcro, he swung his leg wide and walked around the room, talking over his shoulder. "As I was saying, my shift lasts twenty-four hours, which is why I requested someone who can stay overnight. I take it this is okay with you?"

Miss Peach adjusted her black straw hat more squarely on top of her skinned-back gray hair. "Naturally the agency explained your needs in full detail."

"Good. And you're sure four kids won't be too much for you to handle?"

Miss Peach drew herself up even straighter in her chair. "I have been under the employ of the agency for twenty-two years, Mr. Santori. I assure you that I am quite capable of maintaining order and discipline in your household."

At her tone, Danny stopped walking, barely managing to keep his hand from flashing her a mock salute. Suddenly he wasn't sure he wanted to subject his kids to this rigid, humorless woman. The problem was, he didn't have much choice. Maybe he could suggest that she lighten up a bit. He reached down to peel Emma from his leg. "Okay, punkin, the ride's over."

Emma started to resist, but Danny headed her off. "Why don't you find one of Mommy's cups and we'll give Miss Peach a cup of Daddy's special coffee."

Emma brightened. "The purple flower cups?"

"That's right." Danny patted her bottom. "Now scoot."

Emma giggled and scampered through an arched entrance into the adjacent dining room. Danny smiled at Miss Peach and gestured toward an antique oak sideboard. "I keep a pot on all the time when I'm home. Firehouse habit, I guess."

"I don't drink coffee," Miss Peach announced with an imperious shake of her head. "Caffeine, you know."

"Yes, I know. Uh, isn't that the point?" Danny's frown was perplexed, but at her stern stare he added, "Can I offer you something else?"

"Fruit juice, if you have any."

"Sure thing." Danny prayed his refrigerator held something besides Kool-Aid. He went quickly to the kitchen, returning with a plastic pitcher in one hand and his own coffee mug in the other. "I have cherry Kool-Aid—will that do?"

"You have no juice? Juice is good for children, Mr. Santori."

"The kids like this better, I think. It's got lots of vitamin C and stuff."

"Huuummph," was her reply.

He started to speak but stopped short, following Miss

Peach's rapier gaze as it circled the room, cutting across every
surface—or at least what surface could be seen beneath the
clutter. He grimaced at the sight of mail and other papers lit-
tering the coffee table, at the pile of gym shoes tossed hapha-
zardly into one corner, and at the packs of crackers stuffed
around the antique silver service that decorated an old tea
trolley. He remembered how delighted Laurie had been to find
that, and wondered how long since it had been polished.

"Sorry the place is such a mess." Danny shrugged sheepishly. He pushed aside a stack of magazines in order to set the
pitcher and his mug on the coffee table. "The last babysitter
quit rather unexpectedly last week. I called the agency right
away, but I had to work last night...."

"What is that?" Miss Peach pointed to the wall between the
kitchen and dining room.

Danny followed her gaze. "It's a dumbwaiter. One of those
elevator things that comes up from the old cellar where the
summer kitchen used to be. These old houses—"

"I *know* what a dumbwaiter is," Miss Peach replied. "I'm
talking about that."

He squinted at the crack where the dumbwaiter's wood-
paneled door met the frame. Was that a towel wedged in the
opening? Despite his constant warnings, the boys must have
been playing in the thing again. He'd started over to investi-
gate when Emma's chirping voice claimed his attention.

"I found it, Daddy." She emerged from the dining room,
cradling a cup and saucer protectively in her chubby arms as
if they were more precious than gold. "I won't drop it, will I?"

"Of course you won't, punkin." Danny resisted the urge to
snatch up the delicate china, waiting instead until Emma
proudly placed it in his hands. "Good girl."

It seemed a sacrilege to fill the hand-painted porcelain with
cherry Kool-Aid, but Danny didn't care to question Miss Peach's

preference again. He handed her the cup and saucer, then picked up his own coffee mug. "When we're done here, I'll call in the rest of my crew. I'm sure you'll find them a well-behav—"

"AIIIEEEE!" A piercing screech filled the air, followed by the machine-gun-like rat-a-tat-tat of the dumbwaiter door as it slid upward.

Miss Peach jumped to her feet, her arms flying up, cherry Kool-Aid splashing all over the front of her starched white blouse. She managed to hold on to the cup in one hand and the saucer in the other as she stared at the opening in the wall.

From the dumbwaiter's depths two black heads emerged, then two perfectly matched, leering faces. "Earthlings! Surrender. Or we'll slice you open and turn your guts to goo!"

Danny stood frozen for a moment, unsure whether to laugh at the ridiculous sight his twin sons made, kill them or rescue Laurie's china from Miss Peach's death grip. He took a step toward the sputtering woman, then looked over his shoulder at Emma crouched behind a chair with her mouth gaping. "Emma, get some cold water."

"Okay, Daddy."

Danny grabbed a towel from a chair and reached for Miss Peach, intending to blot the spreading stain from her formidable bosom. She batted his hand away, dropping the cup and saucer onto the rug, where they landed with a muffled *thunk.* Her hands now free, she used one to pluck her soaked blouse from her chest and the other to point at the open dumbwaiter. "What on earth...?"

"Come out of there, you two!" Relieved to have something else to do, Danny tossed the towel onto Miss Peach's shoulder, then reached inside the gaping hole and hauled out a pair of identical squirming, mirthful boys, dressed in shorts and T-shirts with aluminum wrapped around their chests to resemble armor. Their older sister's makeup was streaked all over their faces. Tufts of dark hair of varying lengths stuck out at odd angles from their heads, with pink scalp showing through here and there. They must have decided to cut their hair to resemble the alien space warriors they'd seen on an old video the night before.

Danny propped his twin sons against the wall. "Don't move, or the only gooey guts will be yours," he promised.

He turned back to his soaked guest. "I'm truly sorry, Miss Peach. You've probably guessed by now that these are my sons, Kyle and Kevin. They aren't usually so—"

"Daaaaddy!"

Emma's warning cry from the vicinity of the kitchen door erupted just a split second before a resounding *"Woof!"* filled the air. Their huge yellow Labrador retriever skated into the room, paws skidding on the hardwood floor, pushing the Oriental rug up like an accordion. Emma made a valiant attempt to hold the dog's exuberant tail. "Out, General! Sit!"

Neither command was obeyed as the dog leaped toward the two boys. Miss Peach took a step backward, but her sensible low heel caught on a fold of the carpet. Danny grabbed for her, his fingertips just missing her elbow. She flung her arms wide again before falling back into the chair.

"Oh, God," Danny groaned. "Are you all right?"

"Here's the water, Daddy." Emma, holding a sponge at arm's length, raced into the melee and slapped the dripping sponge against Miss Peach's chest. The poor woman let out a strangled cry.

With her eyes bigger than saucers, Emma put one finger in her mouth and backed away. The boys collapsed into a heap, laughing hysterically.

Danny groaned again.

As if pulled up by strings like a marionette, Miss Peach jerked to her feet. She swatted at the dog sniffing the hem of her skirt, snatched the sponge up and flung it to the table, then pointed at Emma. "That was ice-cold, young lady."

Emma burst into tears, which drew her warrior brothers to the rescue.

"Hey," Kyle yelled, his hair sticking out in all directions like a molting rooster. "You can't talk to our sister that way!"

"You better leave us alone!" Kevin added furiously.

General barked an emphatic command before Danny finally gathered his wits enough to respond. "Quiet!" he roared. "Will everyone just…be…quiet!"

The noise level dropped as he turned back to Miss Peach. The woman was a mess. Her blouse was red-stained and soaking wet, her skirt was hiked up to reveal thick stockings and a slip with the bottom strip of lace torn. Amazingly, her hat was still on her head, though it limped to one side.

In a vain attempt at damage control, Danny gestured with his hands spread, palms upward. "Miss Peach, I'm so sorry. What can I say? Boys will be boys."

"Not when I'm here they won't." Miss Peach straightened her clothing. Once in command of herself, she took a deep breath, exhaled through flaring nostrils then bobbed her head with a definitive nod. "It seems my work is cut out for me here. Look around you, Mr. Santori. Usually I do not tolerate such unruliness. Be certain I shall have your children under control in no time. You are fortunate that I am not easily discouraged."

Danny cringed inwardly at the tyrannical tone in her voice; nevertheless, he obeyed her by scanning the chaos around him. But instead of seeing the mess, he saw only the way Emma huddled in the corner, tears in her eyes. Even the boys cowered beneath Miss Peach's smug expression.

He just couldn't do it.

Shoving his hand through his hair, Danny shook his head.

"To tell you the truth, Miss Peach, I *like* a little unruliness now and then."

"Perhaps you don't understand. I just said that I am prepared to give your children the full benefit of my experience. In one week you will hardly recognize them."

That was exactly what Danny was afraid of.

He sighed, feeling like a drowning man giving away his life preserver. "Miss Peach, I appreciate your willingness to take on this bunch," he said, his voice gentle but firm, "but I don't think this is going to work out. Thanks for taking the time to come over."

His declaration was met with stunned silence for a moment, then Kyle let out a triumphant *whoop*. Emma clapped her small hands, her upturned face beaming at him. Even the dog voiced his opinion, his tail thumping the floor in a happy rhythm.

"Well!" Miss Peach clutched her handbag to her stomach. "In that case, I won't waste any more of your time."

By the way her mouth pursed, he could tell her dignity was affronted, but Danny didn't have a chance to make amends before she headed down the hallway for the front door, chin high. He followed, but stopped when she allowed the screen door to slam back, practically in his face.

"Miss Peach," he warned. "Look out!"

Peering through the screen, he watched as she marched down the porch steps straight into the path of Nana, a neighbor's boisterous St. Bernard, who had just dashed around the corner of the house with Alison, Danny's oldest daughter, in hot pursuit. The woman teetered precariously on the last step, then nimbly hopped off into an overgrown flower bed. This time her hat flew off, landing a scant, tempting six inches in front of the surprised dog.

Danny pushed through the door, followed by his three

other children but stopped short of attempting another rescue. Miss Peach stepped forward onto the walk, then snatched her hat from Nana's slobbery mouth. With remarkable dignity considering the circumstances, she looked up at Danny.

"I have no doubt that you will someday regret turning me away, Mr. Santori. In the meantime, good luck finding competent child care. You shall need it." With that she turned and stalked toward her car parked at the curb.

Danny watched her go, torn between feelings of relief and sheer panic.

"Who was that?" Alison asked, snapping her fingers to claim Nana's attention from the flower bed.

"Mrs. Vulcan," Kyle said.

"The Wicked Witch of the West," Kevin added.

"She was *mean!*" Emma exclaimed.

"My last hope," Danny moaned. He rubbed his temple, trying to ward off the headache he could feel coming on. "Well," he muttered, "that went well."

Only Alison, at the age of almost fourteen more astute than the others, seemed to notice the sarcasm. "What will we do now? Dad?"

It was a good question, and he wished with all his heart he had an answer. He tried to summon a reassuring smile. "I don't know, Alison. Will you keep an eye on Emma while I straighten up the mess inside? And you two—go wash up and change your clothes, pronto. And if I ever catch you with scissors or pulling a stunt like that again…" His look had the boys scampering inside like frantic squirrels.

Danny stood on the front porch after the kids had retreated into the house, staring down at the ragged flower beds that Laurie had once kept so neat and orderly. He wasn't exactly a control freak, but lately he had felt just a bit… What was that word? Frazzled? Man, he needed a drink. Or a two-day nap. He needed Laurie. He didn't have time for all of this and work, too. Now, if he could find someone just like Laurie…

He shoved his hand through his hair and sighed. Alcohol and sleep might sound appealing in the short run, but neither would solve his problem. Not when he had to figure out who was going to take care of his kids when his next shift came up day after tomorrow.

What Danny really needed was a miracle.

TESSA DOHERTY WAS in her favorite position, crouched on her knees in the dirt. She whistled happily to herself as she dug her fingers into the soil, kneading and smoothing the flower beds she had designed to enhance the English Tudor house that belonged to her newest client. Reaching for a fairy poly-antha rose, Tessa lifted it from its flat and carefully separated the roots. Gently she nestled the plant into the hole she'd just dug near the low, decorative limestone wall, which would support the delicate blossoms.

"Be happy, little rose," Tessa said, smiling as she patted the soil around the plant. She sniffed, inhaling the pungent scent of dirt newly mixed with fertilizer. To some people the smell was disgusting, but to Tessa the smell was life. It was rebirth and fruitfulness, creation and creativity. The very air breathed hope and new life, which was exactly what she'd needed when she moved from Chicago to Warenton.

Warenton, nestled on the edge of the western Pocono mountain range, was a midsize town, although the locals called it a small city. It was a place where friendly smiles were directed at everyone and a warm welcome was guaranteed. Breaking in to the business market here was a different story. Even though everyone was politely interested and even enthu-siastic about her new landscaping business, they generally pa-tronized the old tried-and-true establishments. She wondered how long she had to be here before she could consider herself a real Warentonian.

Tessa inhaled deeply as the soft breeze brought another fragrant wisp in her direction. Then she chuckled quietly. She could just hear her son's comments if she shared her fanciful thoughts. Eric would probably look at her as if she was nuts and then say, "It's cow manure, Mom. Get over it!"

Tessa shifted her shoulders as she felt a drop of sweat roll leisurely between her shoulder blades. It was hot and humid today. August had arrived with a vengeance. She glanced over at her daughter, Josie, who leaned over an ornamental fish-pond in the center of the garden.

Josie giggled as delightedly as only a seven-year-old could. "Mommy, their mouths look so funny when they eat." She puckered her lips to make a fish face. "Like this."

Tessa laughed. "That's pretty good, honey. Keep it up and we'll have to eat you for dinner."

"Yuck," Eric said. He was sprawled under a tree reading a book. "Josie would taste like a stink-fish."

Josie glared at her brother. "I would not. Would I, Mommy?"

Grinning, Tessa said, "No, funny face, you wouldn't."

"See, Eric!" Josie turned back to splash the surface of the pond as Tessa resumed her work. The garden hummed with bees and the sweet call of birds in the trees. This was the life. Quiet, solitude and hard work to renew her soul. Why hadn't her ex-husband, Colin, been able to understand how important this was to her? How she needed this?

Water under the bridge, girl! Enjoy the tranquillity.

For the next half hour she did. Then she became aware of how quiet it was. There were no sounds from the children, nothing except the twitters of birds and the buzz of insects. Tessa stood up, looking around, but there was no sign of her daughter.

"Josie? Josie, where are you? Eric?"

Then suddenly the silence was broken by the twinkling sound of glass breaking inside the house, followed by a yell. One of the French doors on the terrace swung open and banged against the house. A beautifully groomed white cat streaked out faster than heat lightning. Eric and Josie were right behind the animal, while an astonished Tessa stared.

The kids tried to corner the cat beneath a glass patio table, but the wily animal was too clever for them. The cat feinted right, then left, so Eric bumped into Josie, and in the process, the cat dashed into the shrubbery.

As her children started after the animal, Tessa ordered, "Hold it right there, you two! What were you doing in Mrs. Sherbourne's house? And what was that crash?"

"I wanted to see the kitty," Josie said. "He was sitting in the window."

"I saw Josie go in and went after her. That's when the cat saw the door and made a beeline for outside," Eric explained.

"And the crash?"

"I bumped this big jar by the door and it fell over," Josie confessed with a worried look.

"Oh boy," Tessa breathed. *Mrs. Sherbourne is going to freak.* Tessa glanced around. "Eric, where is that cat now?"

Eric pointed at the shrubbery. "He went that way."

"You'd better find that animal before it wanders into traffic or something worse."

Eric plunged off the terrace into the green bushes, with his sister about to follow. Tessa stopped her. "Oh no, you don't, young lady. Josie, when we get home, you won't be allowed to do anything but go straight to your room."

"Why?" Josie wailed.

"You know why. Didn't I tell both of you to stay out of Mrs. Sherbourne's house? You made a huge mistake going inside when I distinctly told you not to."

Josie opened her mouth to speak just as Eric burst through the wall of clematis and climbing roses that separated the yard from the driveway.

Startled, Tessa lurched around, completely disturbing the plants she had just positioned. "What? Eric, what are you—"

"Grab him, Mom!" Eric pointed to a white blur leaping through the lavender bed.

Before she could move, Eric had followed the errant feline into the flower bed, his feet wreaking havoc as they flattened the delicate lavender blossoms.

"Eric, stop chasing that animal this minute," Tessa yelled, closing her eyes as they both narrowly missed a collision with a flowering pink azalea.

"You told me to find him," her son replied, looking wildly around for the cat as he skidded to a stop on the flagstone path.

"Eeeewww! He's got a poor little mouse." Josie scurried to head off the cat, which was making for a patch of yellow mums.

Tessa leaped up to run interference, but her move only caused the cat to swerve through the flower bed she had just planted, with Eric and Josie close behind, destruction in their wake. "My flowers!"

"We've got him now!" Eric shouted triumphantly... though too soon.

The cat raced for the fishpond. Tessa watched helplessly as her children stopped in time, but the cat misjudged the distance, slipped across the ledge of the pond and plopped into the water. Eric snatched up the furious feline, complete with a wet mouse dangling by the tail from the cat's mouth.

Tessa glanced at the wet Persian cat, who finally dropped the mouse but now was in a snit, spitting, growling and lashing his tail. "Eric, be careful. He might bite."

Inspecting the cat, Eric said, "He doesn't look too happy."

Tessa propped her hands on her hips. "That's an understatement. What did you think you were doing, Eric Doherty, chasing that cat around through my flowers?"

"You told me to find him, Mom. Besides, I couldn't let him eat the mouse."

"Cats are supposed to eat mice. That's their job."

Josie tilted her head. "Did you want the little mouse to die, Mommy?"

"No, of course not, honey. But some laws of nature aren't meant to be broken. *Especially* not on someone else's property, and certainly not when that someone is paying me to landscape her garden." Tessa studied the cat. "That animal is an absolute mess."

Eric looked at the bedraggled white cat, his fur now streaked with mud and sopping wet, his tail twitching with temper. "He wouldn't win any show prizes, would he?"

"Josie, run inside, find a bathroom and grab a towel so we can dry the cat."

"You told me not to go into the house," Josie complained.

Tessa exhaled, trying to keep her temper. "Now you can go into the house."

Josie shook her head as she trudged toward the French doors. "Parents!" A few minutes later Josie emerged with a towel, but she wasn't alone. Mrs. Sherbourne was right behind her.

When the woman reached the terrace she stopped as if she'd been shot. Her eyes darted right, then left before focusing on the squirming cat in Eric's arms. "Prince Puff Puff," she cried, "what have they done to you?" Mrs. Sherbourne rushed to snatch her cat from Eric's arms. "Oh, my poor poor little man, you look like an alley cat." She started to hug the animal but then stopped and held him out away from her while Josie threw the towel over her arm. Mrs. Sherbourne wrapped her precious pussycat in the yellow terry cloth before casting her stern eyes on Tessa.

"Mrs. Doherty, what is going on here? Not only is my cat dripping wet, my flower beds a mess, which I did not pay to have happen, I might add, but—" she paused dramatically "—but my Lalique vase is in pieces on the floor. Didn't I tell you my house is off-limits, especially to children? If you are going to insist on bringing children with you, then I have no choice but—"

Tessa rushed to speak. "No, oh no. It's just been the past few days until I can make other arrangements."

Mrs. Sherbourne looked down her nose at her, something Tessa thought was impossible, but the haughty woman had perfected the technique. "See that you do, please, or I'll have to look for another designer."

"Don't worry, Mrs. Sherbourne, I'll repair the garden. If you tell me the price of the vase I can arrange payments or perhaps free services if that would work?"

Mrs. Sherbourne gave Tessa and her children a frosty glance. "It was a family heirloom given to me by my mother-in-law."

Tessa felt her heart sink at the news. "Oh…oh, my God, I'm so sorry."

Mrs. Sherbourne unbent enough to give her a chilly smile. "It's your good fortune that I have always considered that vase hideous. As for the payment, we'll discuss it later."

Tessa stepped forward. "I can give your cat a bath if you'd like."

"That won't be necessary. I'll call my groomer." Mrs. Sherbourne headed for the house, but looked back over her shoulder. "You'll have the repairs complete by the end of the day, I trust?"

Tessa nodded. "Absolutely."

With a wintry smile Mrs. Sherbourne inclined her head and then disappeared inside the house, leaving Tessa to deal with her children.

"Wow, Mom," Eric breathed. "I thought you were getting fired for a minute there."

Tessa glared at him and then Josie. "No thanks to you two. Take your sister and go to the van. Get some towels and dry off. I'll be right there."

"Mom—" Eric began.

"Right now. And not through the clematis. Go around." Tessa watched her children trudge through a gap in the hedge, then turned to survey the damage in the garden.

It looked as if a tornado had passed through. Uprooted plants lay drying in the sun beside gouges in the freshly turned topsoil. A whole pile of mulch was scattered over the flagstone walk, and the brick edging she had laid so carefully that afternoon was half out of the ground. Tessa passed a hand over her face, wondering how many of the expensive, imported fish were now floating belly-up. No wonder Mrs. Sherbourne was shocked. She'd been expecting her spacious backyard to be turned into a peaceful santuary, not a war zone.

Tessa glanced at her watch. Noon. If she skipped lunch maybe she could— On cue, her stomach rumbled, followed by an impatient honk from the van out front. Tessa sighed. She couldn't get any more work done until she took care of her children. And she might as well grab a bite while she was at it. Hopefully, her best friend Rhonda would be free to watch the kids for the rest of the afternoon.

Just as Tessa stepped around the front of her dilapidated van, Eric pressed on the horn one more time. She jumped, then smiled ruefully, shaking her head at the two grinning children waiting for her. She knew they were good kids, really. It was just that kids and work didn't mix.

To further prove the point, Eric and Josie seemed relieved when she suggested taking them to Rhonda's, making Tessa wonder if they truly enjoyed going to work with her as much as they claimed they did. Had they been trying only to make things easier for her? Josie was too young to understand all the ramifications of the divorce, but certainly at twelve, Eric was aware that their financial situation had changed to a more modest lifestyle.

The van coughed and sputtered as she turned the key in the ignition and eased her foot down on the gas pedal. Sometimes it started right up, sometimes not. Tessa had planned to use the money she made on this Sherbourne job to have the van serviced. Who knew what would happen to her fees now and to her hopes of referrals.

As Tessa ground the van into first gear, a siren wailed in the distance, followed by the commanding blast of an air horn. Even though she couldn't see the fire truck, Tessa pictured the huge red engine barreling to the rescue. Right now she almost wished someone would come to her rescue.

And take away your hard-won independence? Who are you kidding, girl?

Tessa halted the van at an intersection, releasing her shoulder-length hair from its ponytail and running her fingers through the damp strands. Since when had her conscience started sounding like Rhonda? She felt a tapping on her shoulder, and craned her neck to see Josie straining forward against the seat belt.

"I'll help you fix the flowers tomorrow, Mommy."

"Me, too, Mom." Eric nodded with masculine certainty, though his voice broke with a change in pitch. "No more video games at work, no chasing in the garden even if a grizzly bear is chowing down on Josie."

"Hey," Josie protested.

Is this what I want? What good is independence if my kids suffer for it? Tessa turned a troubled frown back to the traffic as the light changed. She hated to see Eric and Josie looking so unhappy, just when it seemed they'd all gotten through the worst after Colin had left. On the other hand, she'd worked too hard to give up yet.

She'd just have to think of something. "Thanks for the offer, guys." Tessa spoke over her shoulder as she moved the van back into traffic. "Don't worry, I'll take care of everything without sacrificing Josie to a grizzly bear." Brave words, she thought as Josie giggled.

All Tessa needed was a miracle.

Chapter Two

Tessa glanced at her watch for the third time, then tipped her head for a better look at the door of the restaurant. Eight-fifteen, and still no Rhonda. Her friend wasn't usually late, but then the vague message about dinner tonight she'd left pinned to Tessa's front door wasn't Rhonda's usual chatty style, either. Thank goodness Tessa's elderly neighbor had been able to watch the kids for a few hours.

Come to think of it, this charming, out-of-the-way restaurant wasn't Rhonda's style, either. Tessa let her gaze wander. Rhonda preferred crowds and places that were ultra hip for their rare dinners together without kids. Mama Gia's was quite the opposite. Worn paneling and intimate nooks lined the empty restaurant while small, cozy tables covered with red-checked cloths were arranged throughout the room. The heavenly aromas of oregano and garlic wafted from the kitchen behind her.

Tessa's stomach growled. If Rhonda didn't show up soon, she might have to nibble on the candle dripping down the empty wine bottle in the middle of her table. Why had Rhonda been in such an all-fired hurry to get together, only to show up late?

Tessa glanced once more at the wrinkled note. "'An answer to your problem,'" she read aloud.

That told Tessa absolutely nothing. The number of problems in her life seemed to be multiplying like horny rabbits. But right now her biggest problem was the growing ache in her stomach. Even so, she couldn't help wondering which of her other problems Rhonda had been talking about. Maybe Rhonda had discovered a way to uncover Colin's hidden financial assets so Tessa could get the settlement she deserved after thirteen years of marriage without costing a fortune in lawyer's fees. Wouldn't that be nice?

Her stomach growled again. Maybe she should start on a salad without Rhonda. Or better yet, some of those mouthwatering buttered bread sticks she'd seen on a table as she'd come in. Tessa leaned forward, lifting her arm to summon the young waiter standing near the menu rack.

At that moment the door swung open and a man walked in. A good-looking man, she noted. He looked around quickly, his head turning her way at the very instant her hand shot up in the air. Tessa froze, forgetting to exhale when his gaze pinned hers.

She almost forgot her hand was stuck up in the air, until she saw his dark eyes widen, then crinkle at the corners. Tessa snatched her hand to her lap, tucking her chin down, but it was too late. He was already weaving his way toward her.

From the corner of her eye she watched his progress through the restaurant with mounting embarrassment and a touch of curiosity. He had dark hair—a bit too long—and smooth olive skin with just a suggestion of five-o'clock shadow. His well-muscled body skirted tables and dodged chairs with graceful ease. An athlete, Tessa thought, keeping her head low. Or just one of those lucky hunks with all the right equipment in all the right places. A shade over six feet tall, he displayed a compact strength beneath a blue knit golf shirt and well-worn jeans.

Next thing she knew, his jeans were so close she could have reached out to stroke them. But as incredibly tempting as that thought was, courtesy demanded she look up instead.

"I'm sorry," she said, offering a tiny shrug. "I wasn't really waving at you. I was trying to order a salad."

A wrinkle appeared between his eyebrows. "You mean you're not Tessa Doherty? You sure look like you're supposed to be."

Her mouth dropped open, partly in surprise and partly at the thrill of hearing her name spoken in the sexiest baritone she'd ever heard. "Huh?"

"Never mind." He rubbed the back of his neck and looked sheepish. "It's my turn to apologize. I thought you were someone I was supposed to meet. I'll get a waiter for you."

"No. I mean…don't do that."

"You don't want a salad?"

"No…yes…I do want a salad, but don't call the waiter just yet." Tessa sighed. She was beginning to smell a rat. "You may as well sit down."

Confusion clouded his expression for an instant, then he smiled. Tessa almost bit her lip at the sight. Perfect, dazzling teeth nearly blinded her, even in the restaurant's dim light. And was that a dimple? A small one, to be sure, but a dimple nonetheless. She had to hand it to Rhonda. She sure could pick 'em.

The gorgeous specimen pulled a chair out and sat down. "You *are* Tessa Doherty, aren't you?"

She raised an eyebrow. "*How ever* did you guess?"

His grin widened as he reached across the table to take her hand. Apparently sarcasm was lost on him.

"Hi, I'm Danny Santori. Rhonda gave me a pretty good description, but you had me going for a minute there. Didn't she tell you I managed to work things out so we could meet tonight?"

His hand was warm and calloused. His eyes twinkled with suppressed humor. A tingling awareness raced up Tessa's arm, halting only when it reached the pit of her stomach. Good Lord, he was attractive! With that wavy dark hair and perfect tan, all he needed was an eye patch and cutlass and he'd be right at home on the set of a classic swashbuckling pirate movie.

"Rhonda didn't tell me a thing." Tessa withdrew her hand, shaking her head reluctantly. "She knows better."

Her cryptic comment didn't seem to faze him at all. He nodded and grinned. "She didn't actually tell me much more than the bare bones of your situation. Only that you're just about as desperate as me."

Desperate? Tessa tried not to let her hackles rise. She was perfectly content with singledom. Only her interfering friends thought otherwise. "Look, Mr. Santini—"

"Santori, but I prefer Danny. I thought Rhonda was supposed to meet us here, but I guess she figured we'd work out the details on our own."

"And what details might those be?"

He tipped his head sideways. One black lock fell over his brow. Tessa had the unsettling urge to push it back. For a moment she wondered if she might be a little hasty to let this one go.

His grin widened. "You know…details like when and where, your house or mine. I've definitely got more bedrooms, but if you're not comfortable with that, we can always try your place."

At that, Tessa's mouth dropped open again. "What— what…" she spluttered. She stopped and pulled herself together. "Mr. Santori…"

"Danny."

"Danny, I'm afraid Rhonda may have given you the wrong idea. I'm not really looking for anyone now."

"You're not?"

"Definitely not. And I have to tell you, I find this conversation moving a bit too fast for me." She grabbed her water and took a quick gulp.

"I have a time crunch. I thought you did, too. I thought we could get business over with and then…"

At his statement, Tessa choked on her water. She started coughing.

"Hey, take it easy. You okay?"

Tessa waved him away. His face clouded over, though instead of diminishing his appeal, it gave him the dark, brooding look of a hero straight off the cover of a novel. Tessa wondered how any man so gorgeous could be desperate enough to agree to a blind date. Probably because his arrogant assumptions turned off every woman he met.

"Just dandy," she gurgled around another cough.

His smile returned, not quite as bright as before but just as lethal. "So it isn't a total waste, at least we can have some dinner and talk. The manicotti here is excellent." He raised a finger to beckon a waiter. He winked at Tessa. "Who knows, maybe I'll change your mind."

Mindful of the other patrons, Tessa placed both palms on the red-checked tablecloth and leaned forward, saying in her most determined yet whispering voice, "Look here, pal, perhaps you didn't hear me. I have enough to handle with two kids and a business. I don't have time for a relationship or…whatever other kind of business you think we're going to do."

His eyebrows almost disappeared into the curls on his forehead. "A relationship?"

"That's right."

"Who the hell said anything about a relationship?"

"You just propositioned me."

"The hell I did."

Tessa wasn't buying it. She crossed her arms and gave him her big bad mom stare. "Then what was all that bedroom stuff?"

Danny clenched his jaw, flushing to the roots of his hair, but whether it was embarrassment or anger, Tessa couldn't tell. "I don't need to proposition strangers to get them into bed. I need a babysitter."

"Then why did you... What did you say?"

Danny overenunciated his words. "I...need...a...baby... sitter. Clear enough?"

Tessa's chin almost hit the table for the third time before she recovered enough to snap her jaw shut. She wrinkled her nose in confusion. "I need a babysitter, too."

"I know. That's what Rhonda told me."

"She did?"

"Yeah, isn't that what she told you?"

Tessa shook her head. "Rhonda didn't tell me anything except that she had the answer to my problem. She's always trying to fix me up, so I thought she meant—"

"A date? With you?"

"Well, you don't have to say it like that," Tessa said, looking around to see if anyone was staring.

"I never accept blind dates. Too risky." A sharp shake of Danny's head emphasized his point.

Tessa crossed her arms over her chest, trying to seem secure and well in command of the situation, but positive she'd just made a complete fool of herself. "I agree," she snapped. Just then the waiter appeared carrying a tray laden with a bottle of Chianti, two glasses, an antipasto plate and a basket of bread sticks. With a flourish he placed them on the table, then leaned over to uncork the wine. "How ya doin', Danny? Put out any fires lately?"

Danny took a deep breath as he slid Tessa a look from under his lashes. "More all the time, Jorgi. How's school going?"

The young waiter rolled his eyes. "Okay, I guess. Already I'm working on Mama's books. But me, I'd rather be a fireman like you, so I can be a hero and have dates with beautiful women."

Danny's deep, resonant chuckle curled Tessa's toes. "Trust me, Jorgi. There are plenty of days when I wish I were an accountant. And this isn't a date."

Jorgi flashed a brilliant smile that showed exactly what he thought of that. "It should be, man. What's the matter with you?"

Danny gave him a stare that had Jorgi hurriedly asking, "You want the usual?"

"Maybe we should ask what the lady wants so we don't have any more confusion. Tessa?"

Trying to regain some dignity, Tessa reached for her purse on the chair next to her. "I'm not very hungry, thank you. I'm just going to—" She started to rise, but her stomach chose that moment to let out a roar worthy of the MGM lion.

Danny sat back in his chair and lifted a quizzical eyebrow. "Not hungry, huh?"

Tessa sat down, placed her purse on the table and busied herself with her napkin to hide her mortification. "Maybe a few bites of something."

"A few bites?" The dimple in Danny's cheek deepened as he smiled. "Bring the manicotti, Jorgi. We'd better feed the woman." The young waiter all but saluted as he sped away. "I hope that's okay with you, or should I call him back?"

Tessa tried to give him a relaxed smile. "Sounds delicious."

"It is and it's Mama's specialty," Danny said. "Look, Tessa, we got started wrong. Let's try again. We can sort this all out while we're waiting. In the meantime," he continued, "have a bread stick."

Tessa threw up her hands. "I have no idea what's going on here, Mr. San…uh, Danny. I thought I was supposed to meet Rhonda for dinner, and instead you show up talking about how many bedrooms you have. Then you say this isn't a fix-up, which is probably good since the only thing we seem to have in common so far is we both have kids—"

"And we both hate blind dates," Danny added solemnly.

"So what are we doing here?" She grabbed a bread stick from the basket he held in front of her and sank her teeth into the perfectly crusted dough. After chewing ecstatically for a minute, she perked up. "God, this is good."

He shoved the antipasto plate closer to her. "You eat and I'll try to explain before you decide to call the cops on me."

As he took a breath to begin, Danny watched her with growing interest. He remembered that Rhonda had mentioned how attractive her friend was, but he hadn't paid attention at the time because it wasn't all that important to him. He sure was paying attention now.

Even though she was sitting down he could tell that Tessa Doherty was tall for a woman, and slender. Her face was tanned a golden hue and the blond streaks in her light brown hair reminded him of the sun setting through the clouds. Her eyes were a warm, true hazel. The unique mixture of green and brown made him think of the earth and growing things.

Except he'd never heard of a wood nymph putting away bread sticks quite the way Tessa did. She was already on her second one.

Danny couldn't believe how fanciful he was getting. He took a bread stick of his own before they were gone. He cleared his throat. "Like Jorgi said, I'm a firefighter. I work out of Firehouse 173. I'm hoping to be transferred to another position in the fall, which would mean a change to more normal hours. Right now I work a twenty-four-hour shift, then have two days off before I'm on again. That's why I'm having so much trouble finding someone to watch my kids. Not many sitters want an erratic schedule or to spend the night, you know."

Tessa gulped down an artichoke and nodded. "I can imagine. You're divorced?"

His eyes shadowed. "Widower. Until recently my wife's great-aunt helped out with the kids, but she's seventy-two and needs hip surgery. She's with them now, but those long hours during my shifts are too much for her to manage. I need to make some other arrangements."

"How old are your children?"

"Alison's almost fourteen, Kyle and Kevin are ten and Emma is almost four."

"Four kids?" She looked startled.

Danny squirmed. "They're good kids. But…they can be a handful. Especially the twins."

Tessa worked her mouth around a black olive. "Mine are twelve and seven. A boy and a girl. And even with two I'm overwhelmed half the time. I'm not sure how anyone can handle more than that."

Her comment made Danny wonder if they were on the same wavelength after all. Maybe Rhonda had her wires crossed. He decided to try a different tack.

"Rhonda told me you own your own business."

"Mmm-hmm. Landscape design."

"Fooling around with plants and stuff, you mean? Do you work full-time?"

"As much as I can. I like to *fool around* with growing things." She glared at him as she picked up a bread stick, broke off a chunk and popped it into her mouth. After a moment she said, "But this is in my busy season, or what should be my busy season. I'm hoping to increase my client list by word of mouth. Not that it's looking too good at the moment. My most recent job was more difficult than I'd expected. I'm not sure my client is going to recommend my services."

"Why not?"

Tessa drained her wineglass. "As a matter of fact she almost fired me over a slight garden mishap that my kids caused. It was really awkward."

"I'll bet."

"She was kind of stuck because her daughter's getting married in that garden and she'd already paid me part of the fee. I had to drop my price to satisfy her, though."

"Tough luck," Danny sympathized as he sipped his wine.

Tessa sighed. "I'll say."

"So who takes care of your kids while you're working?" Danny watched her out of the corner of his eye as he poured them each another glass of the excellent house wine.

"I do—at least I have been since my babysitter moved into a retirement home last month. I can't really afford a sitter right now, but Mrs. Carey and I had an arrangement. I did her shopping and errands and she watched the kids when I needed her, which was most of the summer, actually. Since she moved, they've been going along on jobs with me. That's what caused my problem with Mrs. Sherbourne. No one else has objected but—"

"It's not really working out anymore?"

"Oh, you could say that. Plus, I'd get more done if they weren't around. I end up breaking jobs into two days when I might have finished in one. Still, what choice do I have?" Tessa hesitated, peered at him for a long moment, then muttered, "They were supposed to spend August with their father, but he decided to go to the Bahamas instead with his latest girlfriend—or maybe I should say his latest assistant."

Danny took a slow sip of wine. Rhonda had mentioned Tessa's difficult divorce. He wondered if that was why she insisted she didn't want a relationship, or if, like him, she was simply too busy for the opposite sex.

"One thing about having kids," Danny said as Tessa

snagged another veggie, "you sure can't plan too far ahead. They're always coming up with somethi— Do you always eat like this?"

Her eyes widened, and she gulped down the carrot sliver she had just put into her mouth. "Like what?"

"Like a horde of locusts descending?"

Tessa dropped her gaze to the empty plate and breadbasket, lifted her stricken expression to his, then smiled sheepishly. "Sorry. It's my metabolism. I burn it right off."

"Then it's lucky for you the food's here."

The next several minutes were occupied with Jorgi removing empty plates and arranging steaming platters of pasta and more fresh bread sticks on the table. Tessa sampled the manicotti with a rapturous groan, obviously relishing every bite, while Danny ate more slowly. "I can't imagine where you're putting all of that food," he said.

Once Tessa had slowed down to the point where conversation was possible, Danny pushed his plate away and leaned forward.

"Here's the situation as I see it," he began. "We both need dependable child care. If you'd consider watching my kids during my shifts, I can keep yours for an equal number of hours on the other days."

Tessa looked skeptical. "Six children at once?"

"Why not?" Danny shrugged. "It's not like either one of us isn't used to kids. The more the merrier, my mom always used to say."

"You have *how many* brothers and sisters?"

Danny grinned. "Five, now scattered all over the country. And my mom ruled us with an iron hand. Never a problem."

From the impish twinkle in his eye, Tessa felt certain he was exaggerating, but she couldn't help smiling back. "I'm sure that's true. Still, six children…"

"Only for a day with two days in between—"

"And nights."

"And nights. The other days I'll watch them. What d'ya say?"

His expression was a combination of wistfulness and roguish charm. Tessa wasn't sure which was more appealing, but she knew the intelligent thing to do was to give him an unequivocal no.

"Maybe," she heard herself say, then wondered if it was the wine or the manicotti that had softened her brain. "Can you honestly trust your kids to someone you don't even know?"

Danny frowned. "Of course not. But I trust Rhonda to vouch for you. I first met her at the E.R. on one of my hospital runs. I've known her for years. That's as good as going through a child-care service or putting an ad in the paper. We're getting to know one another now, aren't we? Come on, ask me anything."

Even though Tessa was immediately suspicious of so much undiluted charm, his guileless expression slipped beneath her defenses. A smile nudged her lips. "What do your kids think of this…possible arrangement?"

"I haven't had a chance to tell them yet, since I only talked to Rhonda today. But it might be a good idea to let the kids meet each other before we firm anything up. How's tomorrow?"

"Whoa!" Tessa leaned back in her chair. "I said maybe. I need some time to mull this over."

"I suppose a maybe is better than nothing. How long do you need?"

His dark eyes captured hers, sending another wave of warmth spreading from her cheeks all the way down to the pit of her stomach, which made her uneasy. After Colin she'd sworn off men with charming smiles and dark melting looks.

"I don't know. I'll have to think about it."

Danny gave her a puzzled look. "You have to think about how much time you'll need to think about it?"

Tessa stared at him. "No, I have to think about the consequences."

"What consequences?"

"Are you always this pushy?" Tessa asked in a prickly tone.

"Sorry I'm late, guys." Rhonda's breezy greeting interrupted their conversation and was followed by a loud scraping sound as she dragged a chair over from a nearby table without missing a beat. "The E.R. was packed to the rafters when I left, and no one could figure out how to unjam the computer. I just might have to borrow your Eric someday for that, huh, Tess? Hey, you guys started without me!"

"Tessa was hungry," Danny replied, eyes twinkling.

Rhonda snorted. "So what else is new?"

Since she owed her friend big-time for pulling this stunt, Tessa didn't feel at all guilty about eating without her. "I didn't think you'd make it," she explained. "In fact, I wasn't sure what you had planned for tonight at all. Your message was very brief. Unusually so."

Her thorny comment caused Rhonda to smile crookedly. She spread her fingers through her hair, tousling her short red curls. "That's 'cause I was late already, and only had time to give you the basics after I talked to Danny. No, thanks," she said, waving Jorgi away as he approached with a menu. "I'll just grab something at home." She picked up Tessa's untouched water glass. "The whole idea was just too perfect. I don't know why I didn't think of it before."

"Yeah, perfect," Tessa muttered, eyeing the tray of cheesecakes another waiter carried past their table.

"You didn't think of it because you didn't know about my aunt's surgery until I ran into you at the E.R. last week," Danny pointed out. "But Tessa's not sure she even needs child care."

"What are you talking about, Tessa?" Rhonda flapped a napkin open on her lap. She picked at the parsley garnish which was almost the only thing left on the antipasto plate and turned to Danny, jerking a thumb in Tessa's direction. "She told me she wished Eric and Josie didn't have to go with her to work because they're bored to tears, but they'd be worse off stuck in her dinky condo all day. She told me she'd give anything if they could go someplace where they had room to play and other kids to play with."

A scowling Tessa pointed a finger at herself. "Sitting right over here, guys."

"What else did Tessa tell you?" Danny asked solemnly. Only the humorous glint in his eyes and the twitch on one side of his mouth gave him away.

"She said she wanted them to be safe." Rhonda turned to Tessa. "How much safer can they be than with a fireman? He's a trained EMT, for God's sake!"

"Oh!" Tessa gave an exaggerated jump. "Sorry, were you talking to me?"

"Did Tessa tell you how much she loves kids?" Rhonda asked, pointing at Danny with a piece of celery. "She used to be a den mother, and a volunteer at Josie's preschool a few years ago. She's great at organizing games and outings so that everyone's happy. When you said you were looking for a new babysitter, the whole thing just clicked in my head. And now that you've met, everything's settled, right?"

Her unhampered, unflagging optimism was one of the things Tessa loved about her friend. It was also one of Rhonda's most annoying traits, depending on the day. Today it was annoying.

"It's not as easy as that," Tessa replied. "I have to—"

"Think it over, right?" Danny said.

His voice sent another shudder through Tessa's midsection. No man deserved to be so sexy. This could definitely be a problem, she thought.

"So what's the problem?" Rhonda asked, as if she'd read Tessa's mind.

Danny looked at her in silence.

"There's no *problem*," Tessa insisted. She felt her cheeks warming beneath the double scrutiny. "I said I'd think it over and I will, but I'm not sure this is what's right for my kids just now. Look, Rhonda, I appreciate your concern and the trouble you went to, but I am an adult and would appreciate it if you didn't try to order my life or push me into anything. I've had enough of that, thank you very much. My ex-husband saw to that."

For the second time that evening Tessa reached for her purse. She knew she was acting like a total idiot, rushing out like this, but she didn't like being pressured into things too fast, because she always felt she made bad decisions when she did—and Rhonda knew that.

Tessa opened her wallet and tossed a couple of twenty-dollar bills on the table to cover her share of the meal. Then she stood. "Look, my kids are waiting at home. It was good to meet you, Danny. I'll let you know what I decide."

Danny stood politely as she backed away from the table. She made the mistake of looking into his eyes. They glittered like polished stones, only warmer and softer. His head tilted slightly to one side, his expression a mixture of curiosity, appeal and unabashed interest.

She thought he might try once more to convince her, and braced herself. But only a little. With a jolt, she realized she wanted to be convinced.

Instead he only flashed her a grin. "It was nice meeting you, too, Tessa. Rhonda has my number in case you're interested."

Tessa smiled back, because she couldn't help herself. He had that kind of smile.

"You can't leave yet," Rhonda said, throwing up her hands in disgust.

"I'll call you tomorrow, Rhonda." Tessa marched toward the exit, excruciatingly aware that Danny was watching her retreat. Rhonda's incredulous voice followed her as she escaped through the door.

"I don't believe this! She left without even having dessert."

Chapter Three

Tessa pulled to the curb and sat for a moment trying to get her nerves under control. Though there'd been little traffic on the streets at this hour, her heart raced as if she'd just maneuvered through an obstacle course and her cheeks felt warmer than the early-morning temperature warranted. She gripped the steering wheel to stop the slight trembling in her hands.

Too much caffeine, she lied silently.

In order to calm down, she forced herself to study her surroundings—not a difficult task at all. She loved these old neighborhoods with their fake Tudors, and soaring Victorian monstrosities. The yards were large by any standard—an acre or more each—and the trees were massive. Old neighborhoods were definitely the best, she thought, exiting her van. Even when they were rather shabby.

Spotting the address Danny Santori had given her on the phone last night, Tessa walked up the path that led to a huge, wraparound porch with a welcoming double leaded-glass door set in the exact center. She stopped and stared.

Shaded by a pair of oak trees that allowed the sunlight to spill onto the yard in dappled diamonds, the Victorian home in front of her possessed that effortless aura of dignity and authority that upstart modern homes would never have.

The paint had faded to a soft, uneven blue and the white window frames were flaking a bit, but that didn't detract from the enchanting two-story bay tower that anchored one side of the house. Several high peaks on the roof looked made for a pair of mischievous squirrels to slide down on a frosty day.

"Oh, my," Tessa breathed, delighted by the warmth emanating from the home. This was the kind of house she'd always wanted her kids to have. Forgetting some of the hesitation she'd felt earlier, she stepped forward, taking care not to trip over the weeds growing between the cracks in the walk. She stopped for a closer look, brushing her hand over the small green leaves nestled happily between two flagstones. Not a weed after all. She closed her eyes at the fragrance. Thyme. The herb had spread from the plants that bordered the sidewalk on each side.

She plucked a sprig and tucked it into her pocket before continuing toward the broad white steps of the porch. Glancing to either side, she was dismayed at the overgrown and neglected landscaping. Someone had once started to make a difference here, then allowed it to slide into a jungle. Her fingers practically itched to sort through the perennials. But first things first.

Tessa climbed the steps, her gaze wandering from the old-fashioned swing occupying one corner of the porch to the newer white wicker chairs and round table hugging the tower in the other corner. She reached for the dull brass knocker on one of the doors and lifted it, letting it fall with a ringing thud. The sound was so lovely, she tried it again.

The door jerked open beneath her hand.

Danny Santori stood before her, but she hardly recognized him as the same man she'd dined with the other night. His eyes were heavy lidded and his black hair stood off his head in tufts.

"Who…? Oh! What are you doing here?" He shoved one hand through his hair, making it stick up even more.

Tessa frowned, not so much at his abrupt greeting as to suppress her own reaction to his rumpled—but oh, so sexy—appearance. "You invited me, remember? When I called last night."

"You said you'd stop by in the morning."

"Right." Tessa pointed to her watch. "That's now."

Danny grabbed her arm and peered at her wrist. "It's only seven-thirty, for God's sake. I expected you at some civilized hour, like ten, maybe."

Tessa pulled her arm away, giving him the once-over. He must have rolled out of bed only a few minutes before. His face was shadowed with black stubble and his eyes were still at half-mast. A T-shirt was partially tucked into low-riding jeans so old and faded they seemed to be part of him. His bare feet hugged the floorboards.

Despite herself, she couldn't resist a smug grin. "You're not a morning person, are you?"

Danny rubbed a hand over his face. "What makes you think that?"

"Wild guess."

He smiled then, a lopsided twist of his lips that made Tessa's own lips automatically tingle. Maybe it was the dimple. Really, the guy could make money off that smile. How else could she explain her reaction?

"Uh…may I come in?"

Danny backed up, waving her inside. "Oh, yeah…sorry."

Tessa stepped into a foyer that fulfilled all the house's promise of welcome. Huge pocket sliding doors lined the ample rooms to the right and left. A grand staircase arched up to the next floor. Tessa eyed its sweeping lines, picturing a Victorian lady descending in flowing satin. She stepped forward to stroke the wide banister.

"It's so smooth."

Danny chuckled. "Not from polishing. More likely from the bottoms of all the kids who've slid down it over the years."

Tessa considered the curve. "You're right. It has the perfect width and slope."

"Be my guest."

She chuckled. "Maybe when I know you better."

"That was the first thing my wife Laurie did when we bought this place."

Tessa wasn't sure what to say, so she said nothing. His voice held no bitterness—only a hint of amusement laced with tender longing. The moment passed quickly. He touched her elbow, indicating the dining room through the archway to the left.

"Sorry. Coffee, I've gotta have coffee. Want some?"

Tessa preceded him into the dining room and took a seat at the scarred oak table. "I'm not sure I should have another cup. I've already had two."

Danny paused before the sideboard with a mug in one hand and the coffeepot in the other. "Really? When did you have the time?"

"I usually get up at five."

"Good God," Danny sputtered, nearly dropping his mug. "Why? I can't even move much before eight."

"That's my time to think. Time to plan the day and get myself geared up to tackle it. But I don't understand. You said you work twenty-four-hour shifts. How can you do that if you can't get yourself going in the morning?"

He shrugged. "That's different. That's work." He took a sip of coffee. "So does this mean you've changed your mind?"

Tessa blinked and realized she'd been staring at him. "About what?"

Danny gave her a strange look. "Are you sure you didn't get up too early? After all, you called me."

"Oh, right." Tessa fought to keep from squirming. "I guess I'm willing to talk more about this arrangement, provided the kids are all okay with it and we can work out the specifics."

"The specifics?"

Tessa nodded. "I have several questions."

"Okay." Danny took a long swig of his coffee, then rolled his shoulders as if to loosen up. "Fire away."

Tessa pulled a short list from her hip pocket. "First, I'll need to know exactly which days you work so I can schedule my jobs around them."

"No problem. I'll give you my calendar. There could be a few things that fall outside what's listed there, but we can work it out. What else?"

"Second, we work out a food budget. You shouldn't have to pay for all the meals that my kids and I eat here."

"We don't have to—"

"Yes, we do." Tessa lifted her chin a notch. She thought she detected a smile hidden behind his coffee mug, but accepted Danny's nod of acquiescence.

"Third, we agree to give fair notice if either of us wants to change the arrangement. Say, two weeks?"

Danny swallowed and lowered his mug. "I have no intention of backing out on you."

"I didn't think you would, but you did say you're hoping for a job change. Who knows what might happen then?"

"That's true," he admitted. "I'm hoping for that to come about when two of the guys in the department are offered an early-retirement package, though I'm not sure of the timing." His mouth twitched. "Are you going to back out on me?"

"Of course not," Tessa protested, tracing a swirl in the oak tabletop with one finger. "I just think we should understand each other, that's all."

Danny lifted an eyebrow. "Oh, I think I understand. But I'll agree with all your rules. Anything else?"

"One more thing." Tessa pretended to study her list while she avoided his eyes. "What are your plans for sleeping arrangements?"

He smiled. "Did you have something specific in mind?"

Tessa sent him a narrow look. "Are you flirting with me? There's no flirting—that's part of the ground rules."

"Flirting? Of course not. I just figured that because you seemed so prepared…" He indicated her list.

"Hmm." The glint in Danny's eyes left Tessa wondering.

"Sleeping arrangements. Well, I've got one extra bedroom fixed up that you can use. Your kids can either sleep in the loft on the third floor or in with my kids if they want. I hope that's okay. There are two more bedrooms that I use for storage, but they need some fixing."

"Good…that's fine. I mean, I guess that answers all my questions." Tessa nodded. Risking a glance at him, she half expected to see that roguish grin she'd encountered at the restaurant, and was surprised to see a solemn expression. It was almost a disappointment.

Before she could examine that unexpected thought, a small figure bounced in through the doorway leading from the kitchen, tattered blanket trailing.

"Hi, Daddy."

"Mornin', punkin. You've already been into the peanut butter, I see."

Tessa hid a smile as the adorable little girl in her peanut-butter-streaked nightie hugged Danny's knees.

"You were talking to the lady, so I had to do it myself."

He patted her tousled golden hair. "Why didn't you eat some cereal?"

"'Cause Kevin wanted peanut butter sammiches for the camp."

"What camp?" Danny pried his daughter from his legs. "Are your brothers up in those trees again, after I told them not to?"

"They're not." The little girl shook her head so fiercely, her lopsided ponytails—which looked left over from the night before—bounced. She put her finger in her mouth and stared at Tessa.

"Tessa, this is Emma. This is Mrs. Doherty…."

"Tessa's fine."

He smoothed Emma's sticky hair. "She might bring her kids over and be your babysitter while I'm working. Can you say hello?"

Emma removed her finger from her mouth with a pop. "Hi. Where are your kids?"

Tessa smiled at the sweet round face. "They're home eating their breakfast now." She glanced up at Danny. "Eric's at that age where he thinks he's old enough to stay home alone. I've started leaving them for short periods once in a while. But I should get going soon."

Danny nodded. "Alison doesn't think she needs a babysitter, either, but I can't see leaving her with all this responsibility yet. She's not even fourteen."

"I will be in a few weeks, Dad," proclaimed a sulky voice from behind Tessa. "You keep forgetting that."

Tessa turned to watch the teenager round the newel post on the staircase. Alison had the same golden sweetness as her younger sister, though her curves were beginning to show up in other places. She plopped onto a chair near her father and swung her long coltish legs over the arm. She fixed a suspicious glance on Tessa, obviously questioning her reason for being there.

"Dad thinks I'm still a *child!* But I'm not."

"All fathers think that," Tessa admitted, exchanging a warm

smile with Danny before bringing her gaze back to Alison. "Mine does, even now."

"I *don't* need a babysitter. And we don't need a babysitter for anyone else, either," she said with a pointed expression as she glanced at her dad and then back to Tessa.

"Alison…" Danny's voice sounded a low warning, but Tessa headed him off, recognizing the sense of ownership in the teenager's eyes. She knew she'd have to tread carefully with her.

"That's good to know. I was worried about whether six kids would be too many to handle. Five sounds a little better, and I could sure use your help."

Alison hunched a shoulder and appealed to Danny again. "Dad, really, I think we should talk about this."

Danny had picked up a paper napkin and was wiping peanut butter from Emma's face. Instead of answering he changed the subject. "Alison, will you get your sister some breakfast? I'll round up the boys so you can meet them before you leave, Tessa. But how about dinner tonight with the whole gang? We can talk more then."

With a friendly smile at Alison, which was met with a perfunctory nod, Tessa stood. "Sounds good to me. Where?"

"McDonald's," Emma chirped.

"But I'm supposed to meet Bethany at the mall tonight," Alison complained.

At that moment the room erupted as two boys burst through the kitchen door. "Hey, don't we get a choice? We want pizza!"

Astonished, Tessa could only stare at them. They were as boisterous and identical as two blackbirds fighting over a crust of bread. They'd already been out in the dirt, she could see. And both had the strangest haircuts…. Tessa looked back at Danny and smiled. "They look like you."

"I have more hair at the moment," Danny muttered. Then he corralled the pair and made quick introductions. "So Kevin and Kyle want pizza, Emma wants burgers—what do your kids like?"

"That depends on what day it is," Tessa replied. She glanced down at Alison, whose mouth was pursed in a sulky pout. "How about the food court at the mall? That way everyone can eat what they want and then play in the arcade afterward."

"Yippeee!" The boys didn't wait around for further discussion. Emma clapped her hands gleefully, and even Alison appeared happy with the decision as she led her younger sister into the kitchen.

"The mall it is." Danny escorted Tessa to the front door. "Six o'clock?"

She stepped out onto the porch, turning back just in time to see Danny struggling to hide a yawn. She couldn't resist teasing him. "Six is fine…if you think you'll be completely awake by then."

"Maybe she changed her mind."

Danny stopped scanning the crowd of shoppers surging past the food court and glanced down at Kyle, who squirmed impatiently.

"Probably she's just combin' her hair or somethin'." Across the table, Kevin aimed a packet of ketchup at his brother and smashed it with his fist. Fortunately, the packet remained intact.

Danny intercepted the ketchup before his son could try again. "What makes you say that, Kev?"

"That's why Alison's always late."

"Nope, I don't think she's comin' at all," Kyle repeated slyly. "I bet she changed her mind just like all those other babysitters. She took one look at that big zit on Alison's forehead and ran screamin' for the hills."

"Little creep," Alison muttered, slouching in a chair at an adjoining table in a vain attempt to pretend she was an only child.

"Daddy, is that true?" Emma's eyes widened solemnly. "Did Tessa change her mind?"

"No, honey." Danny patted Emma's head with one hand and lightly cuffed Kyle with the other. "She's just a little late, that's all."

"Well, I wish she'd hurry. I'm starvin'!"

Danny silently agreed with his son, though not for the same reason. The thought of seeing Tessa again made his pulse pound just a little faster than usual, not to mention the fact that keeping all four kids gathered in one spot wasn't easy. Lifting his head, he peered toward the mall entrance.

"I think I see them," he said a few moments later after spotting a woman Tessa's size as she angled through a cluster of teenagers loitering in front of the music store. "Wait here. Alison, keep an eye on these guys, please."

Danny covered the length of the food court in long strides, dodging a couple of boys as they raced toward the arcade. Halfway across, Tessa looked up. Her smile deepened, sending a shock wave through Danny's gut.

"Sorry I'm late." She stopped directly in front of him, allowing a group of ambling shoppers to move around them. A bright-eyed little girl skipped behind her. Tessa indicated a dark-haired boy, who followed more slowly. "I forgot that Eric had a baseball meeting."

Danny smiled back at Eric, who was all arms and legs. "You play baseball?"

"Sort of. I'm not very good."

Tessa put her arm around his shoulder. "You will be. I just need to find more time to practice with you, that's all."

Eric rolled his eyes and shrugged her arm away. "No offense, Mom, but you stink worse than me."

"Nobody stinks worse than you, Eric," his sister said in a matter-of-fact tone as she skipped just beyond her brother's reach.

"Josie, don't be rude."

"Motormouth," Eric countered.

"Hey, you two, put a lid on it." Both kids pouted, but they obeyed. Hands on her hips, Tessa sighed dramatically. "Well, here they are."

Josie butted her head around her mom to peer up at Danny. "Hi, I'm Josie."

"Hi, yourself. You can call me Danny." He leaned down to squeeze her hand. She was a miniature Tessa, from her honey-colored hair to the sun-kissed freckles dusting her cheeks.

Josie pointed past him. "Are those kids yours?"

Danny glanced over at his children, who were, remarkably, watching from the same place he'd left them. "Yep. Wanna meet them?" He was speaking to the air, however, because Josie was already skipping her way over to the table.

Tessa shook her head. "My extrovert. Now Eric, on the other hand…"

"Mom, don't talk about me like I'm not here."

"Sorry."

Danny watched the boy blush, then reached out for a handshake. "You know, Eric, I played some baseball in college. Maybe I could give you some pointers or something."

"That'd be great," Tessa answered. "Wouldn't it, Eric?"

Eric sent his mother a sidelong glance. "Maybe."

"Why not—"

Danny stopped Tessa with a hand to her shoulder. He'd been a boy once, and knew what it was to be embarrassed about something and wanting a girl to stay out of it. Especially his mother. "It's no big deal. If you're ever interested, just let me know, okay? Let's go meet the troops."

"Okay," Eric mumbled, looking relieved.

Danny led Tessa and Eric back to the table, where Josie was already engaged in conversation with Emma and Alison. Eric took a seat to one side, but the twins were not about to let him keep to himself. The noise level gradually increased. After allowing them a few minutes to get acquainted, Danny had to whistle to gain their attention. "Who wants what to eat?"

"Pizza!" the twins shouted in unison.

Eric shrugged. "That's all right with me."

"Me, too," Josie chimed in.

"Me, too," Emma repeated imitating Josie.

Danny turned to Tessa after Alison had also nodded in agreement. "We'd better get the pizza before they change their minds. Why don't you help me play waiter?"

They left the chattering group and weaved their way toward the pizza counter. Danny glanced back once, but none of the kids seemed to notice they'd gone. "That's funny. Emma's usually shy, but she's talking away to Josie."

"As if she'd get a word in edgewise." Tessa laughed. "Eric is shy, too, but he seems okay with Kevin and Kyle. It's a good thing they're not all shrinking violets."

"You might wish they were in a few days," Danny commented. "My house gets pretty noisy with my four around. But six might raise the roof. By the way, do your kids eat like you do?"

Tessa punched his arm playfully. "Not quite. You're not changing your mind now, are you?"

"No...just wanted to know how many pizzas we need— eight or nine."

"Two large pepperoni pizzas, please," Tessa said to the waiting clerk with a smile. "I can always eat something when I get home."

"Make that three large pizzas, then." He grinned at Tessa. "I don't want you to go home hungry."

After placing their order, Danny watched Tessa gather napkins and straws onto a tray with quick, efficient movements. She moved with such easy grace and innate confidence that he found it hard to believe she was as unsure of herself— and as vulnerable—as Rhonda had implied. "Not worried anymore about handling six kids?"

"A little. Aren't you?"

Danny shrugged. "I told you, it'll be a piece of cake."

"A piece of cake? Oh, you naive man."

"Okay, a piece of very messy cake." At Tessa's chuckle, he added, "I hope you'll give this arrangement a try. I think we'll make a good tag team."

Tessa gave him a quizzical look as the clerk slid three large boxes across the counter. Danny scooped up the pizzas while Tessa followed with the drink tray. They were met with a cheer. "Better stand back," he added to Tessa as he placed the boxes in the middle of the table and flipped open the lids. "Here you go, troops. Dig in."

"Talk about a feeding frenzy." Tessa shook her head. "I didn't realize they were all so hungry." She slid into a chair near Emma and reached to help the little girl separate a piece from the rest without losing all her cheese.

"I like macaroni," Emma piped up.

"That's *pepperoni*, dummy," Kevin said.

Alison moved her chair close enough to grab her own slice. "Look who's the dummy. You just got sauce all over your shirt."

Tessa helped Josie to a serving, then looked around the table. "Everyone else all right?"

"Dad needs some," Alison pointed out. However, when Tessa reached for a plate, the girl snatched one up and put two pieces on it. "I'll do it. Here, Dad. These are the two biggest."

Danny sighed. "Thanks." He had wondered if Alison would begin defining her territory, as she had before with his occasional female friends. She'd already fired the first shot when she met Tessa at the house. He'd have to explain to his daughter that this was not a date. Just because Tessa was forty years younger than his last sitter was no reason for anyone to forget that this was strictly a business relationship. *Especially him*. The problem was every time he saw Tessa he found himself wanting to forget it.

He glanced over at Tessa, who, after a wry look, obviously chose to ignore Alison's possessive behavior. Her usual sunny smile was in place as she lifted a piece of pizza to her lips.

Mesmerized, Danny watched as she closed her eyes to inhale the spicy aroma. After a few tentative nibbles, she opened her mouth wider for a bigger bite. Her pink tongue darted out to lick a bit of tomato sauce from her lips.

Suddenly Danny's collar felt too tight. Good lord! If she made eating a pizza look like a sensuous experience, he wondered what making love to her would be like.

"Is that okay, Dad?"

"Is it?"

Dragging his attention away from Tessa, Danny looked over toward his twin sons. "Huh?"

"Eric said he'll show us how to beat Blasterman. He knows all about that computer stuff." Kyle gave the older boy an admiring look.

Danny could scarcely nod his approval. He was still trying to figure out how he'd nearly drifted off into a sexual daydream in the middle of the mall, surrounded by six kids. He reached into his pocket for a handful of change and passed it over. "Don't leave the arcade. And stay together," he added as the three boys raced off.

"I have to go to the bathroom," Emma said, tugging on his elbow.

"I want to play skeeball," Josie insisted.

Before Danny could respond, Tessa slipped Emma's hand into hers. "I'll take your sister to the bathroom if you'll help Josie with skeeball," she said to Alison. "I'm not very good at it."

"Good idea. Alison's an expert at skeeball. Just until your friend shows up, okay, Ali?" Danny hoped to head off any impending protest. He forked over another bill. "Use the change machine."

He leaned back to watch Tessa walk away with Emma, enjoying the view nearly as much as when she'd first approached. Her shapely backside swayed provocatively, and even in the artificial light of the mall her hair shone golden as she leaned closer to Emma.

Realizing what he was doing, Danny turned his attention toward cleaning up the table. He busied himself with throwing away the empty pizza boxes and then checked on the boys before sitting back down to wait for Tessa. Of their own accord, his thoughts centered on her mouth, and how much he wanted to see if her lips were as soft as they looked.

Hold on there, you jerk.

He mentally shook himself, wiping furiously at a spot of pizza sauce on the table. If he wasn't careful, he'd wind up scaring her off for sure. She'd said she didn't want a relationship. Neither did he, but in the past few days he'd thought more about his love life—or lack of one—than he had in years. Maybe it *was* time for him to start dating again.

"My daddy doesn't sleep in his underwear 'cause he says he's too big." Emma's high-pitched voice penetrated the din of the mall, bringing Danny's head around to meet Tessa's surprised look as they neared the table.

She was struggling to control her expression, but a huge grin won out. "Because he's too grown-up, don't you mean?"

Emma shook her head. "No, too big."

Danny groaned. Kids were so literal. He racked his brain to remember what else he might have said that Emma could repeat.

"Do you wear your underwear to bed?"

Now that Emma's interest had shifted, so did Danny's. He watched a blush rise from Tessa's collar to her cheeks.

"Well...not exactly."

"'Cause Daddy says you're gonna sleep with him at our house."

Danny rolled his eyes and stood up to face Tessa. "I didn't say it quite like that."

Tessa laughed. "Don't worry. Josie was three once, too. And she's still way too inquisitive for her own good."

Danny grinned back and lifted Emma and threw her over his shoulder. "Okay, punkin, we've had enough questions for one night. Let's go ride the merry-go-round. Coming?"

They crossed the mall quickly. Once Emma was safely strapped onto the ride, Danny stepped back to Tessa's side. "The kids seem to be getting along." He hesitated, not wanting to seem pushy. "And I hope you can tell by now I'm no serial killer."

"I'm not sure what you are, but I *do* believe I can trust you with my kids." Tessa brushed a wisp of hair from her cheek and smiled up at him. "I guess we can give it a try."

Relief washed through Danny, along with a few other emotions he refused to acknowledge. "That's great. There's only one thing, though. I had every intention of taking the first turn just to show you I'm a stand-up guy, but that was a few days ago. My schedule was changed and a few duties added that we have to talk about, but the problem is that my next shift starts tomorrow morning at six. If you want to wait, I'll understand, but..."

"But you'll be up a creek without a paddle." Tessa nodded. "That's okay. I'll start first."

"Thanks. You're a doll."

"I feel more like a guinea pig." She gestured toward the three boys in the distance, hunched conspiratorially in front of a video game. "Or more appropriately, a sacrificial lamb."

She was kidding, of course, but as Tessa watched Danny wave to his youngest daughter, she couldn't help but wonder at the funny feeling in her stomach every time she looked at him. Or thought about him.

The last few years of her life with Colin had been enough to turn her off men, no matter how sexy and appealing they were. But being around Danny made her feel exhilarated. Excited. Hopeful.

And that's what scared the hell out of her.

Chapter Four

The next day at exactly 5:20 a.m. Tessa walked down the uneven walk to Danny's house. She adjusted her backpack stuffed with overnight clothes and hiked a bag of groceries higher as she tried to avoid catching her toe in the cracked concrete, plus keep two half-awake children in tow.

"Jeez, Mom, it's the middle of the night," Eric grumbled as he fiddled with his MP3 player.

Tessa cast a glance at the headphones that adorned his ears. She could swear the kid slept in them. "Not too early for music, though, unless that's a lullaby playing in your ears."

Eric stopped dead and sent her such a horrified look that she was tempted to give him a big kiss. There he stood all bones and angles except for the sweet curve of his jaw that reminded her of the fluffy bear he used to sleep with. His dark eyes were still drooping with sleep, and his hair stuck up like a porcupine. She suddenly felt such an overwhelming rush of love for him that she wanted to cry.

Eric scowled at her. "Do I have toothpaste on my nose or something?"

"No." She shifted the weight of her groceries and hugged him quickly, ignoring his pull to get away. "You look like a skinny teddy bear this morning."

"Ewww, gross!"

Josie hugged her pillow and leaned against Tessa for a moment. "How come we had to come so early?"

"Because Danny's a fireman and he has to go to work." Tessa stroked Josie's soft hair, dropped a kiss on her forehead and then started them moving toward the front doors once again.

Tessa grimaced when an overgrown weed still covered with cool morning dew slapped across the top of her foot. She stepped closer to the porch and cast a professional eye over the hydrangea bushes. They were too leggy and left like that they wouldn't bloom anymore, which would be a crime, as they'd probably been there forever. It would be a shame to lose them through neglect. She couldn't stand it. Right then and there she decided to weed and prune this afternoon.

She glanced behind her as she climbed the steps. "All right, you guys, hurry up. I think Danny needs be at work by six, not leave at six. We might need to come earlier next time."

Tessa ignored her children's groans and turned at the door to thrust the grocery bag into Eric's arms. She pulled the backpack off her shoulder and thrust her hand inside the pouch to find the key Danny had given her. She inserted it into the keyhole and turned the knob. Bumping the glass with her hip, she held it open and gestured Eric and Josie inside. Tessa quickly followed them and felt her breath catch in her throat. The inside looked delightful, as if the house was throwing out a welcome for its visitors. Early-morning light streamed through a small leaded and stained glass window on the stairwell, falling in refracted patterns of color on the parquet floor. The staircase gleamed, the light covering its rich mahogany patina like a soft blanket.

But the best was yet to come. Danny appeared at the top of the stairs and slowly descended, still tucking in his shirt.

Tessa caught her breath. This was yet another version of

Danny. Stronger, more purposeful, his clean-cut jaw firm with decision, his strong arms set off by short sleeves, his blue eyes enhanced by the deep dark shirt, the pants falling snugly from his trim waist, hugging his hard thighs.

There was something about a guy in a uniform!

Danny stopped as he noticed them standing in the hallway. Caught by her intense stare, he instinctively responded by dropping his gaze to check his zipper. Tessa swallowed a chuckle as he looked up and with a rueful grin said, "Hi."

"Good morning. I hope we're not too late."

He checked his watch and continued down the steps, his composure restored. "Nope. Right on time."

"I've never seen you in uniform before. Very impressive."

His eyes gleamed. "You think?"

A tingle raced down her spine as she met his gaze. She found that rather alarming, so she turned to drop her backpack onto a table in the foyer, then said in a light tone, "Sure. Now I know why little boys want to be firemen when they grow up."

"I don't want to be a fireman," Eric muttered, slipping his headphones down around his neck.

Danny descended the rest of the stairs. "Any other ideas, Eric?"

Eric grinned. "How about a baseball player?"

Danny gave Eric a teasing punch on the arm. "From what you told me, you'd better think again."

Josie piped up. "I'm hungry."

Danny grabbed his hat from the hall tree and then turned to cup Josie's chin in his palm. "You were so quiet, I thought you'd lost your voice."

Josie wrinkled her nose. "I don't talk all the time."

Eric rolled his eyes. "Yes, you do."

Josie propped one fist on her hip, clutching her pillow with the other. "Do not."

Tessa caught Danny's gaze and pursed her lips. "I think these two just woke up."

Danny indicated the staircase. "Mine are up but strangely quiet, which is probably my cue to leave."

Tessa nodded. "Maybe I can get another cup of coffee under my belt before I have to deal with six kids at once."

"All you have to do is survive for twenty-four hours, then I'll take over for the next forty-eight. Piece of cake!" Danny walked to the door. "Help yourself to anything you'd like. *Mi casa es su casa.*"

Tessa followed Danny as he opened the door. "In that case, you won't mind if I pull a few weeds?"

"Knock yourself out!" He smiled, adding, "I know it's a bit of a mess. My wife was the gardener."

Tessa cast another glance at the overgrown landscape Danny called a yard. "No kidding."

Just as Danny started to say something, World War III erupted in the upstairs hallway.

Alison's angry voice fired the opening shot. "Did you two get in my purse and take my note?"

Tessa and Danny looked at each other, then glanced up at the second-floor landing to see Kyle and Kevin standing shoulder to shoulder as they faced their sister. "We didn't get in your dumb old purse."

"You did, too. My note's gone and I know I put it right in the pocket, 'cause I read it last night."

"Then how could we have it?"

"You came sneaking into my room when I was taking a shower."

"No, we didn't."

"Uh-huh, you did, too." Emma stumbled into view, rubbing her eyes as she headed into the uproar. "You said you were robbers."

Danny stepped toward the stairs, then swore under his breath as he checked his watch. "I'm gonna be late."

Tessa pushed him toward the door. "Go. I'll handle this." *I hope,* she added silently.

Danny hesitated for a moment, then backed up. "I wouldn't want a fire to start without me."

Tessa shooed him toward the door. "Piece of cake, remember?"

Danny backed onto the porch. "If you're tempted to kill the twins, you've got my permission. They're starting to eat too much anyway."

Tessa laughed. "I'll remember that."

Waving goodbye, she shut the door. Then, feeling like a raw recruit, she turned to take command of the battleground. Tessa set her sights on familiar targets first.

"Eric, take the groceries into the kitchen. Josie, put your pillow and things in the living room for now, then help Eric unload the bag." She watched her kids for a moment before taking a deep breath and marching toward the stairs. The noise was deafening as she drew closer, since Danny's kids were still discussing the situation at the top of their lungs.

Tessa leaned casually on the railing. "Trouble?"

Alison threw her an angry glare before turning her attention back to her brothers. "Not after I kill them."

"Ohh," Tessa said, making sure an apologetic tone stayed in her voice, "afraid I can't let you do that. I'd have to clean it up, you see."

Startled, Alison glanced back at her. "They took something that belongs to me."

"Then I don't blame you for being mad, but you still can't kill them." As Tessa looked at the two boys, she wondered how she'd ever be able to tell them apart.

"They're my brothers—I can kill them if I want to."

Kyle and Kevin thrust their chins forward belligerently. "No, you can't."

"Who says?"

The twins turned and pointed at Tessa. "She does."

For a moment it looked like a standoff, then little Emma came running back down the hall with a piece of paper waving in her hand like a flag of truce. "I gots it, Alison."

Alison plucked the note from Emma's hand. "How'd you know where to look?"

"They put everything in their old catcher's mitt."

The twins turned outraged faces to their little sister. "You been snooping in our room?" Kyle, or Kevin, demanded. Well, whoever it was, Tessa thought, it was time to put a stop to the entire battle. They all needed a breathing space—and so did she!

"All right, we'll get to the bottom of this later. Right now, boys, why don't you get dressed. Alison, put your note away, please, and then you can help with breakfast if you'd like." Tessa's glance fell on Emma, who was shifting from foot to foot. She smiled. "Emma, you'd better go potty right now." Staring at the kids, Tessa waited for a moment…a long, tense make-or-break moment. Would they obey her or run over her like a tank battalion? Everyone stood still except Emma, who dashed into the bathroom and slammed the door. Then the boys shrugged and trailed back to their room. Meanwhile, Alison carefully folded her note and avoided Tessa's gaze.

"You know, Alison, I had an older brother who was a real pain." Tessa palmed Alison's shoulder and squeezed. "It gets better."

Alison stiffened at her touch. "When?"

"When they get around thirty." Tessa grinned at Alison, her spirits rising when Alison gave her a small smile in return.

Alison rubbed her toe on the carpet, peeking at her under

her lashes. "Part of the problem is I don't have my own room. I have to share with Emma."

Surprised, Tessa looked around the large Victorian house. "Why not? Your dad said there are two extra bedrooms here plus the loft."

"Who knows?" Alison said with a shrug. "I want the loft, but Dad ignores me when I hint at it. He thinks I'm still a baby."

Tessa dusted her hands ready for action. "Well, why don't you show me the loft and we'll see what we need to do. Then I'll clear it with him."

A satisfied look spread across Alison's face. "You'd do that?"

"Sure." Tessa nodded, then started down the stairs saying over her shoulder, "Right after breakfast, okay?"

That didn't go too badly, she thought as she entered the kitchen. Eric and Josie had lined up the groceries on the counter.

"Hey, Mom, I thought you said you'd just got a few things for breakfast."

"I did."

Josie indicated the loaded countertop. "We're going to have all this for breakfast?"

Tessa nibbled her finger as she studied the eggs, sausage, bacon, bread, bananas, melon and orange juice. "I didn't know what everyone liked. So I thought I'd make a few extra things."

"There's enough here to feed an army," Eric commented.

"Six kids will probably eat like an army," Tessa muttered under her breath as she moved to the counter and opened a few drawers and cupboards to familiarize herself with the kitchen. She handed a bowl to Josie and a frying pan to Eric. "Let's get going. The rest of the troops will be arriving any minute."

Twenty minutes later Tessa and the kids were assembled in the dining room. Each child stared incredulously at the table groaning under mounds of scrambled eggs, French toast, bacon, sausage, fruit and a pitcher of orange juice and carton of milk.

"Wow—French toast!" Kyle said.

Tessa passed the plate of fried bread. "Dig in, Kyle."

"I'm Kevin. He's Kyle."

Tessa turned to stare at the other twin, who regarded her with owl-like eyes. "He is?"

Emma giggled. "No, he's Kevin."

Tessa could feel a headache starting as she stared from one twin to the other. "Who's Kevin?"

She tried hard to keep from grinning as each boy pointed at the other.

"I see," said Tessa. She leaned forward and studied them intently. Although both boys had the strangest haircuts she had ever seen, one had a huge V cut out of the front. If she could just find out who it was, she might have a chance. "I've been meaning to ask—what happened to your hair?"

Emma chomped on a sausage, talking around it. "They played space alien attack."

Tessa pointed at the twin on the right. "I'll bet it was Kevin's idea to cut their hair, right?"

Alison met Tessa's eyes and slyly indicated the twin on the left, the one with the cutout V. "Nope. Kyle's."

"Ahhh." Tessa stared at Kyle and wondered if he was generally the instigator. Seeing his twinkling eyes, she had a feeling she'd hit the bull's-eye. He looked like an absolute imp! She passed a platter of bacon to him. "Here you go, Kyle, eat up."

"We usually have cornflakes," Alison said.

"So do we," Eric responded with a shy smile. Tessa watched Alison smile back and relax enough to take some eggs along with her fruit and toast. For the next few minutes the only sound in the dining room was chewing and a strange sort of snuffling. Tessa paused as she passed the plate of French toast to the twins again. "What's that noise?"

Kyle and Kevin suddenly put both hands on the table and looked like angels, which instantly activated Tessa's nerves to red alert. "I'm talking about that noise that sounds like a pig inhaling."

Eric, caught unaware with a big gulp of milk, swallowed a laugh, which turned into a gulp and a coughing choke. Alison, with Josie's help, got up to thump him on the back. Then to Tessa's horror, the tablecloth started to slide to the side, as if pulled by a tractor beam. She grabbed it and held on. "What the—"

Emma disappeared under the table. "General, let go."

Tessa flipped the tablecloth up and bent to stare at the huge yellow Lab, who greeted her with a happy lick right on the mouth. She straightened in a hurry and picked up a napkin. "Blech!"

Alison reached under the table and hauled General out to the kitchen, saying over her shoulder, "Dad told you two not to feed the dog when we're eating."

"That was the dog making that noise?" Tessa asked after Alison had pushed General out through the dog door.

Emma nodded. "He was the babiest puppy, so he had to gobble his food. That's why he's so noisy—right, Alison?"

"Right."

Tessa grinned. "Well, at least you don't have a pig." She stood and started to collect the dishes. "If you'd all help clear the table, then you can go out and play, or whatever, okay?"

Kyle and Kevin nudged each other. "We can work on the camp." They grabbed their dishes and disappeared at high speed to the kitchen. They skidded to a stop and called to Eric. "You can come if you want. We're going to dig a hole."

"Okay," Josie said, sliding off her chair and scrambling after Eric.

"Not you," Kyle said. "Dumb old girls aren't allowed."

"I'm not a dumb old girl."

"All girls are dumb," declared Kevin.

Tessa waited for a moment to see how Josie would handle the situation. When Eric didn't help and Josie seemed too surprised to move, Tessa was compelled to jump in. "Josie knows more about digging holes than anybody. She helps me all the time."

"Forget it," Josie finally said. "I don't want to come to your dumb old camp." She flounced back to the table. "I want to stay here with Alison."

"Men." Tessa sighed as the three boys, with satisfied smiles stretching their faces, tromped out the back door. She exchanged knowledgeable glances with the three girls staring back at her. "I remember my brother doing the same thing to me." She poured another cup of coffee and saluted the group. Emma and Josie grabbed their milk and lifted their glasses high in response and Alison dropped her sulky teenage attitude long enough to do the same. "Here's to the women of the house, who see no reason to dig a hole in the dirt."

"Unless you want to plant a flower," Josie added.

"Precisely." Tessa took a sip, letting the hot restoring liquid trickle down her throat. "After we clear the tables, I think we should find a new room for Alison. What do you say, girls?"

The rest of the day passed semi-smoothly, except for one small problem when the twins convinced her that they were allowed to use Danny's tools on their camp. When she discovered the truth from Alison, Tessa put a stop to it and after apologies all around she decided not to mention it to Danny. She reminded herself to talk to him about Alison's room situation instead. Day passed into night, and soon everyone settled down to bed.

That evening Tessa sat in the living room with a book and listened to the creaks of the old house settling around her.

There was comfort in the soft music of the leaves and the clicking of the branches as a breeze stirred the big old trees that surrounded the house, comfort in the buzz of the insects outside the screens, in the soft hooting sound of a night hunter as it perched in the leaves and waited for dinner, in the shimmer of friendly shadows that reclined in the recesses of the room. Tessa stroked the arm of the faded chintz armchair.

Strange how some places can immediately twine around your heart and feel like home.

She noticed a picture in a silver frame standing on the mantel. She closed her book and crossed the room for a better look. Danny and a lovely woman laughed back at her. The love and contentment in the picture reached out and grabbed her. Thinking back, she couldn't remember her married life ever holding that much uninhibited joy.

"You were so lucky," she whispered.

Her eyes were drawn to Danny as he stood braced against the wind on the deck of a boat. A funny little flutter, like a moth trapped in a jar, brushed her stomach. She hadn't had that type of response for long time, in so long that she backed up, distancing herself from the picture as if Danny was in the room. A chuckle escaped at the absurdity of her action, before her gaze returned to Danny and she picked up the picture again. She studied the protective way his hand cupped his wife's shoulder, the smile in his eyes and the way his posture reflected his complete contentment.

I wonder what it would be like to have him look at me like that.

Alarmed at that thought, she replaced the picture on the mantel. *Enough of this. Time for bed.* Heels clicking briskly on the oak floor, she left the room without another backward glance, even though she could still feel Danny's smile reaching out toward her, calling her back.

AT SEVEN O'CLOCK the next morning Danny quietly let himself in the front door. The house was silent, so silent that he wondered if he'd come to the wrong one. It wasn't unusual for his kids to sleep a bit later in the summer, but he would have thought with new kids spending the night, they might have gotten up earlier.

He removed his hat and hung it on the elaborately carved hall tree, then placed his bakery bag on the seat. After unbuttoning the top buttons he peeled his shirt over his head, rolling his shoulders and letting the cool air play over his bare skin, enjoying the freedom. He was reaching for an old shirt hanging on a hook when he felt it. Someone was watching him. He turned, shrugging into the shirt and leaving it open, and spied Tessa standing in the middle of the stairs, one hand on the railing and the other at her throat.

For a long moment time froze as Danny stared up at her, taking in the long line of her tan legs emerging from the bottom of her shorts. Finally, shaking his head like a wet dog, he grabbed the white paper bag and walked to the bottom of the steps. "Hi."

Tessa lowered her arm. "Hi."

Danny lifted the bakery bag clenched in his fist. "I brought a surprise. Fresh bagels."

Tessa descended, stopped on a step above him and sniffed. "They smell delicious. Where'd you get them?"

"A little bakery I know. My dad used to take me there as a kid." Danny took her hand and tugged until she stepped onto the floor, grinning as she almost stumbled into him. Unable to resist, he dropped a casual arm around her, guiding her toward the kitchen. He needed to make contact with her. He didn't examine why. After seeing her this morning he just knew he had to touch her, needed to smell the fresh-flower scent of her hair, to see the spattering of freckles that sprinkled her pert nose, to hear her laughter, but most of all he wanted to taste her skin to see if it was as creamy as the buttermilk it resembled. He'd thought of her last night but didn't dare tell her, so he told her about Mr. and Mrs. Kreigler instead.

"These bagels are handmade by an old German couple. They've had this bakery on the far side of town since they both came to America about sixty years ago. I like to stop by and say hello, make sure they're all right, that sort of thing. It's not the greatest neighborhood anymore."

Tessa looked up at him. "Danny Santori, the protector, right?"

He smiled. "It gets to be a habit—protecting things, I mean."

Tessa slid from under his arm and went straight to the coffeepot. "Oh, I don't know if I'd call it a habit. Habits are something you develop. I think it's more likely who you are inside."

Danny followed her, sniffing the rich aroma of freshly brewed coffee. "Hey, you made coffee?"

"The kids told me how you like it—strong with a pinch of cinnamon. I didn't want you to come home tired and have to make it yourself, so I set the timer for automatic."

Danny leaned an elbow on the sideboard. "Now who's protecting who?"

Tessa shook her head and reached for a cup. "Making coffee has nothing to do with that. It's simple courtesy." She poured them both a cup, handing one to him. "Besides, if I remember right, you're not a morning person. If you're going to deal with six kids—and animals—today, I thought you might need it."

Danny took a sip. "There weren't any alarms last night, so I got a great night's sleep. How about you?"

She shrugged. "Strange beds, you know. Don't worry, I'll be fine."

"How'd you make out yesterday with the kids?"

"Not too bad. I didn't get to the gardening, though." She

set her mug on the table and walked into the kitchen, returning with plates, knives and cream cheese. "Why don't you break out the food before my taste buds curl up and die?"

Danny sat down, tearing open the bag to expose the golden-brown beauties. The yeasty scent hovered in the cool morning air, making his mouth water. "I love these things."

Tessa slipped into a chair and reached for a blueberry bagel, then slathered it with cream cheese. She took a bite, swallowed, then closed her eyes, savoring the taste. Slowly she ran her tongue over her lips to find the excess cream cheese.

Danny gulped. "Uh, you missed a spot."

Once again her tongue went into action before she opened her eyes and sent Danny a look that made his gut tighten. "I've never tasted anything so good."

Danny could think of a few things he could offer, but his promise to keep their relationship businesslike, plus the rules of polite behavior, kept his mouth shut.

"Do you bring these home every morning?"

"No, just for special times. Laurie and I used to get these bagels as a treat when we were first married. Then it became a celebration tradition. This is your first morning here after watching the kids and spending the night, so this qualifies."

"Thank you. I appreciate the gesture." She took another bite and closed her eyes as she chewed. "It's just as well we don't have these every day. I'd end up the size of a barn."

Danny smiled. "An attractive barn, though."

Tessa reached for his hand, taking Danny by surprise. He started to say something, but she only turned his wrist up to see his watch. With a squeak she inhaled the rest of her bagel and downed her coffee.

"I've got to go," she said as she started to collect her plate and coffee.

Danny half rose from his chair. "Leave it. I'll get it."

"Okay." Tessa tucked her dark green polo shirt more firmly into her khaki shorts.

"I like the uniform," Danny said. He pointed to the patch over her breast. "That's the name of your company, Living Lifestyles?"

"Well, the company's only me, but I didn't want to be Tessa's Plants or something cutesy like that."

"Well, it sure sounds interesting. I thought you'd have a rough, tough, weed-killer sort of name."

Tessa put her hands on her hips. "Are you making fun of me?"

"No. Just commenting."

"I don't think about gardening that way. I'm into living, not annihilating." She arched her brow. "Look, Danny, as much fun as it is, I don't have time to debate my company's name with you. I have to be at the Sherbournes' house by seven forty-five or she goes ballistic."

"Is that client still giving you some trouble about the kids' damage?"

"Not since I gave her that break on price and offered more free services to help pay for her damaged vase. But I don't want to push my luck, since a referral to her friends could bring me some more business."

Danny nodded. "Well, have a good day."

Tessa backed up to the hallway. "I should be back by eight tonight. Then we need to talk about a couple of other personal things, okay?"

Danny's heart jerked at that comment. "Personal? Such as?"

"I'm sorry, but I can't go into it now. I'm late." With a brief wave, Tessa disappeared, leaving Danny to stare after her.

He took another sip of coffee. "I wonder what she meant by personal?"

His mind leaped in all directions as he considered the possibilities of those words. Now if his day went smoothly, and there was no reason it shouldn't, he'd make sure he was showered, shaved, relaxed and ready to talk about anything she wanted to talk about, before he steered the conversation into a few of those directions that were beginning to occur to him every time he looked at her.

THAT EVENING DANNY SAT in the porch swing, with Josie beside him talking a mile a minute while he dotted antiseptic on her knees and reflected on his "smoothly running day." What a vain hope that had been. He dragged his attention back to Josie, who hadn't taken a breath since she'd joined him on the porch.

"You know what they said then? Then they said—we told you no girls allowed."

"That's when you and Emma decided to take the camp, eh?"

Josie nodded so hard her hair bounced. "We got some sticks and started beating the bushes and thumping the ground—"

"To scare the boys?"

"Then I fell in the hole…and I thought I'd never get out, 'cause I couldn't reach above my head 'cause it was too deep, and it was all covered over with sticks, then Kyle and Kevin leaned over and yelled—"

"No girls allowed?"

"They said it served me right for falling in their girl trap and they had them everywhere and if I ever tres—tres—"

"Trespassed?"

Josie nodded. "Yeah, then they'd leave me there until my skin dropped off and my bones were white, but I'd have long hair 'cause it would keep growing…."

Danny gave her a fascinated look. "It would?"

That's all it took to keep Josie going for another five minutes. At the end of which Danny had capped the bottle of disinfectant and slapped some colored Band-Aids on her knees. He'd been really tempted to put a few over Josie's lips at the same time just to get a moment of peace.

"So…do you think even boy ghosts have long hair, huh? Do you, huh?"

Before he could answer, Josie continued her monologue. Danny ran his hand around the back of his neck. His muscles felt like iron and his temples throbbed. *God, how does her mother listen to this child all day long?* Not that Josie wasn't a good kid…she was just exhausting. He wanted to lean back and take a nap. Maybe if he just nodded at the right moments she wouldn't notice.

"Hi, Mom," Josie yelled, her voice echoing off the porch ceiling.

That's when Danny's head really exploded. Who would have thought babysitting six kids would be so exhausting? After all, he already had four. Two more should have slipped in with no problems whatsoever. It hadn't worked out that way, though. He swiveled to squint at Tessa coming up the walk at a brisk pace. From her swinging stride and broad smile she'd obviously had a better day than he had.

Josie jumped off the swing and raced to the steps in time to throw herself against her mother and hug her around the waist. Tessa tilted Josie's face and kissed her nose. "Hey, jelly face, did you have a good day?"

"We had peanut butter and jelly for dinner, with malted milks. That's Danny's favorite."

Tessa looked over at Danny. "That sounds nutritious."

Danny groaned at her censorious look, then tried to defend himself. "Well, I'd intended to have hamburgers, macaroni and vegetables, but by the end of the day…"

By the end of the day he'd wanted to kill the whole damn bunch of them, including the dog! He'd had only enough energy to slap down some bread, the almost empty peanut-butter jar and a crock of jelly and tell them to help themselves.

Tessa grinned as she looked him over. "Aren't you the one who told me this would be a piece of cake?"

Danny sat up a bit straighter, trying to ignore his stained T-shirt, old torn jeans and holey gym shoes, remembering how he'd intended to wow Tessa with his charm when she got back. Unobtrusively he tried to push his hair back from his forehead, surprised when his hand seemed to stick.

"Yuck, you've got peanut butter in your hair," Josie said as she glanced over at him and giggled. "Now it's sticking up. You look like a porcupine."

Danny watched Tessa trying to hold back a grin as she stopped Josie from running over to clean him up. He groaned. So much for his suave and debonair image.

"Maybe you'd better get your things together and find your brother. We have to get home."

"Okay." Josie waved at Danny and raced inside, banging the door behind her.

Danny winced at the sound before making a supreme effort to smile. " Have a good day?"

Tessa nodded, the glint in her eye very pronounced as she answered, "Mmm-hmm. Did you?"

"Before or after Hurricane Kyle-Kevin-Emma-Alison-Eric-Josie hit?"

Tessa laughed and threw herself onto the swing next to him. "That bad, huh?"

Danny grinned. "Well, they just seemed to be everywhere at once—like ants. Ants with loud mouths."

Tessa snorted. "Now you know what stay-at-home moms put up with every day."

"Well, now I know what stay-at-home dads have to put up with, too." He wiped his hand on his jeans. "There's probably a good lesson in all of this. I'm just too whipped to figure out what it is."

"I already told you." Tessa laughed. "Never have more kids than you have hands."

Danny laughed, too. "I'm beginning to think you're right. I know I sure don't understand what's gotten into everyone today."

Tessa set the porch swing moving with her foot. "What do you mean?"

"Alison."

"Ah, she told you about the room? That's what I—"

With an accusing stare, Danny said, "Told me about it? No, I wouldn't say that. She informed me that she now had a new room. That you said she should have her own room and that she was too adult to sleep with her little sister anymore."

Tessa stiffened at his tone. "I didn't exactly say that."

"No? Then what did you say?"

"I just agreed with her that she was old enough for her own room and that a house with so many extra rooms should be put to…" Tessa trailed off before hunching a shoulder. "I guess I should have talked with you first."

"Oh, do you think so?" His voice dripped with sarcasm. "You might be right. Maybe you should have talked to me about my daughter before you rearranged my life. Especially since I specifically told her that we will discuss the loft after she's gotten settled into high school."

"She didn't tell me that. She indicated you wouldn't talk to her about it." Tessa exhaled, trying to control her annoyance as she realized she'd just been duped by a savvy young manipulator. She'd have to be more alert from now on.

Danny waved his hand. "Forget it. It's done. I'll cope, but my little girl is all alone up there on the third floor. She might as well be sleeping on the roof tonight," he muttered.

Tessa struggled to contain a smile at his dramatic tone.

"I'm sorry. I thought it might break the ice a bit if I were to help her. But remember I told you I needed to speak to you about something personal this morning."

"You wanted to talk about Alison?"

"Partly, but… What were you thinking I wanted to talk to you about?"

"I don't know. Personal generally means something to do with me. You have something to do with me, so I thought you meant something to do with me and you." He groaned inside at the idiocy of that statement. This woman was already confusing the hell out of him.

Tessa frowned. "You and me? You and me…personally, you mean? I do have something to discuss, but it's kind of hard to…Why are you looking at me like that?"

Was she really that unaware that he found her attractive? A swift glance away and a flush on her cheeks reassured him that she was as conscious of this unexpected current between them as he was. His good humor suddenly restored, he decided to quit teasing her.

"You could have warned me that I was expected to move furniture all day as part of my child-care duties."

Attention diverted, Tessa exclaimed, "Oh no, you didn't move the furniture already? Now we'll have to pile it in the middle of the room to paint."

"Who's painting? The loft doesn't need painting."

Tessa eyed him as if he'd just beamed in from a lost planet. "No, not if you like that bilious shade of greenish-yellow that someone slapped on the walls."

"I don't think it's so bad."

"It looks as if a grasshopper spit on it."

Danny squirmed. "It came like that. I just left it because—"

"I know. Alison was too young for her own room. Well, she does need her own room now. She's a teenager."

Danny shoved his hand in his hair again. "I still don't understand the big deal. My brothers and I slept in the same room."

"Girls are different. Their own space is very important to them."

"Why didn't she tell me that?" He sighed. "She used to confide in me."

Tessa patted his hand. "Don't worry, she will again."

"I don't think so. She's mad at me."

"Why?"

"I answered the phone."

Tessa lifted an eyebrow. "So?"

"It was for her, but I said she couldn't talk because she was folding her underwear."

Tessa collapsed against the back of the seat and hid her face in her hands. Her voice was muffled as she gasped, "You didn't?"

"Well, I didn't know it was a boy. His voice was so high-pitched—at least at the beginning it was—I thought it was a girlfriend." He ignored Tessa's gurgling sounds. "I mentioned the underwear, then said 'Rob who?'…then all hell broke loose! Alison flung herself down the stairs, grabbed the phone and told me she'd never speak to me again." He reached over and shook Tessa's shoulder. "It's not funny!"

Tessa lifted her face, now streaming with tears. "I'm so sorry, but…" She couldn't say any more. Danny waited for her to get control of herself.

"The damn kid's not even fourteen, which means I have six more years of her as a teenager. What am I going to do?"

"Freeze her until she's twenty-one?" Tessa suggested.

Danny laughed, his outrage rapidly disintegrating as he watched Tessa's smiling face, marveling at the play of emotions that swept over it. "Good idea." He hesitated then touched her nose with the tip of his finger. "You've got a few more freckles from the sun today. They look like fairy dust."

Startled Tessa drew back. "I, uh—"

He continued to trace her cheek. "You have a few here, too."

"Never mind my freckles," Tessa brushed his hand away, then changed the subject. "I got a lot of work done today. I think this will work out well."

Danny smiled at her, grinning more widely as she struggled not to respond. "While we're on the subject, you mentioned another personal item you'd like to share?" He tucked a tendril of hair behind her ear. He couldn't help himself; he wanted to touch her again.

"I'm not sure now's the time."

Danny smiled again, setting the porch swing moving with his foot. "Sure it is. It's a lovely evening. Time to settle back and relax."

Tessa smiled. "Yes, it is, unfortunately…" Tessa indicated her clothes. "We're both covered with dirt and I'm kind of hot and thirsty, so it can wait."

Danny indicated a nearby table featuring a tall glass sweating in the leftover heat. He picked it up and offered her a sip. "I just happen to have a glass of watered-down iced tea I'm willing to share. So ask away."

Tessa took a sip before tucking some stray wisps of hair behind her ears. "I noticed Laurie's picture last night. You both looked so happy."

Danny wasn't prepared for Tessa to bring up Laurie. Thinking about the woman he'd lost over three years ago was getting much easier, but he wasn't used to speaking about her to anyone. It was a wound he had closed over and buried deep. Since meeting Tessa he was beginning to emerge from his personal darkness. He wasn't sure what that meant, either, so he treated it with flirting and teasing until he could figure it out.

"I'm so sorry, Danny. I didn't mean to upset you."

"No, no, that's okay. We were happy. Very happy."

"Can you tell me what happened to her?" At Danny's look, Tessa said gently, "I'm not trying to pry. I'm only asking because if one of your children talks about her to me I'd like to know what to say."

Danny was quiet for a moment, wondering how to describe the woman he'd fallen in love with in high school to this woman he was finding himself drawn to in the present.

"I know she was lovely," Tessa prompted.

"My Laurie was very lovely, inside and out." He was still for a moment before continuing in a quiet voice. "She was warm and giving and energetic, never even caught colds, so when she was diagnosed with cancer we didn't believe it."

"When was that?"

"Laurie was pregnant with Emma when they discovered the tumor. It had spread by the time they'd discovered it. She had an option of chemotherapy and other medications, but they couldn't guarantee the baby wouldn't be affected. Laurie refused to even consider the subject. She thought she could make it until after Emma was delivered and then she'd start treatments. We were hoping the disease wouldn't spread rapidly." He took a sip of his iced tea before saying, "We were wrong."

"I'm so sorry, Danny. She must have been a remarkable woman. I can't imagine how hard it must have been for both of you."

"We fought over her decision about the treatment, but Laurie dug in her heels. I wanted her to live, and she was determined to do so. She said she'd be the exception to the rule. She lived until Emma was six months old and then God had other plans for her, I guess."

"So Emma didn't get a chance to know how wonderful her mother was, did she?"

"No, and the boys were little and don't really remember that much. It's been hardest on Alison. She and Laurie were very close. Laurie called Alison her flower fairy when Alison was little."

"She sounds incredible."

"She was. We first met in elementary school and by our senior year in high school we were pre-engaged. I went on to college and Laurie worked as an administrative assistant, but the minute I got into the fire department she gave it up. She said she wanted to focus on home, our family and me, since I had such a demanding career. That's the type of long-term relationship I needed. Still need. Before Laurie died she made me promise that I'd marry again, but I..."

"Couldn't," Tessa said, blinking hard.

"It's hard to find someone who will put her family first, put me and the kids above anything else. That was Laurie. She was the strongest woman I've ever known."

"Thank you for sharing this with me."

Danny turned and stretched his arm along the back of the swing. "What about you, Tessa?"

"Me? Me what?"

"How long have you been divorced?"

"A year and a half next month."

"Don't you want to get married again?"

"Why?"

"Huh? Well...uh...I don't know. Most women want to be married, don't they? Get married, have a family?"

"I've been married and I have a family. To tell the truth, I didn't always like my marriage. It was always all about my husband, and not about my needs. After a while that didn't work for me anymore, so I finally did something about it. Now I have my children and I've started a business I love, so I don't know that there's much marriage can offer me."

"Are you off men, too, or just marriage?"

"I find men—some men—attractive." She glanced at him,

and then just as quickly glanced away. "I'm not dead, just divorced. But I don't know that I want that type of complication. I'm not looking for involvement."

Danny pretended to wipe his forehead. "Whew! That's a relief." He wasn't sure what to make of Tessa yet and he was a man who liked straightforward answers. This woman puzzled him, and that annoyed him. It also threw him off balance.

"You look tired, Danny. I can make it a bit later tomorrow if you'd like, say at nine? That way you can sleep in."

"Sounds good. Thanks."

"Does your head hurt? You're squinting your eyes as if your head hurts. Do you have a headache?"

"Don't go all motherly on me," he snapped with an annoyed look.

Tessa drew back at his tone. "I wasn't trying to…"

Danny waved away her explanation. "Never mind. You're right. Sorry, my head is killing me."

Tessa dug in to her pocket. "Would you like some aspirin? I have some right here."

"No, I'll be fine. I just need some more sleep."

"Okay. See you tomorrow."

Danny's head started pounding again as Josie slammed out of the door, with Eric right behind her. He watched Tessa usher the kids to the car, looking even more appealing in the twilight as the last rays of sun highlighted her hair. The sight affected him more than he expected and he groaned, sprawling back down onto the porch swing. *You'd think I'd never seen a woman before.* He raised a feeble hand as Tessa honked goodbye. He could see trouble coming.

Right now he wished he'd never heard of Tessa Doherty, or her family.

Chapter Five

Tessa glanced at her watch as she and her children trudged up the sidewalk to Danny's. She was earlier than she'd said she'd be—eight-fifteen instead of nine o'clock. She hesitated before turning the handle and stepping inside. The house seemed very quiet, unusually quiet.

"Where'd they go, Mom?" Josie whispered.

"Maybe aliens took them. Better watch out." Eric muttered. poking his sister in the ribs.

"Shhh," Tessa whispered, her finger to her mouth. She looked around. "I guess they're still asleep."

"Wish I was asleep," Eric grumbled.

"You shouldn't have stayed on the computer all night," Josie said.

"I didn't."

Josie plastered a smug look on her face. "Did, too. I peeked under the door and saw the light."

"Eric Doherty, were you on that computer after I said lights out?"

Eric glared at his sister. "Tattletale."

As Josie started to reply, Tessa jumped in again. "Never mind, we'll talk about this later, Eric. And Josie, I'll speak with you later also about spying on your brother. Now both of you go upstairs and get some more sleep." Convinced her stern mother act had them suitably cowed, Tessa turned and headed toward the kitchen.

A few minutes later Danny tracked her down there. "I smelled coffee."

Tessa jumped and spilled a few drops of hot coffee on her hand. "Ouch. Warn me next time."

Danny reached over her shoulder to grab her hand and thrust it under the cold water. "Sorry, I didn't know you were going to scald yourself."

With her back against him, Tessa felt his flesh on hers as their legs touched and she jerked forward, slamming her hip against the counter. "Ouch."

"What are you trying to do, kill yourself this morning?"

"What are you wearing?" Tessa demanded.

"I'm not wearing 'jammies,' if that's what you're asking," Danny teased as he released her.

"You'd better be wearing clothes," Tessa said over her shoulder as she tried to recover her aplomb, although the sensation of his hard body against hers was still with her as she went back to pouring coffee into her cup.

"Why don't you turn around and see?"

Tessa sighed, then turned and surveyed the ratty bathrobe falling open over a pair of running shorts and a T-shirt that said Firemen Burn Hotter. Her lips quirked into a smile she quickly controlled. Danny Santori didn't need any encouragement to be outrageous.

"Nice shirt. And even if you don't sleep in jammies, you own a bathrobe, I see."

Tessa took a sip of coffee, screwing up her face as the liquid burned her tongue. *What is it about this man that keeps me tripping over my own feet?* She glared at Danny, daring him to make another comment, but he studiously ignored her, walking past to get a coffee cup from the cupboard.

"You said you weren't coming until nine."

"I know. I'm sorry. I forgot that I have an appointment with a vendor, so I had to come early. Where are your kids?"

"We were all up late watching a movie. Then Emma was crying because her big sister was living in another room and didn't love her anymore. After I settled her down, the boys decided to make a commando attack on Alison's room to scare her. That started another uproar, and then—"

"I get the picture," Tessa interrupted.

Danny poured coffee and leaned back against the counter, looking both at ease and very sexy at the same time. "So what time will you be home?"

"Home?" There was silence for a moment as Tessa met his eyes before correcting him. "Oh, here to get the kids, you mean? About seven-thirty." Tessa winced as she recognized the tone as the same one she'd used with her ex-husband when he was pushing her to do something she didn't want to do.

"See you then."

Walking toward the hallway, Tessa nodded and waved, still feeling Danny's gaze boring into her back. She'd known what he meant, but the little tingle in her stomach at the word *home* made her curl her emotions up in a ball like a porcupine. She almost ran to her car, knowing that if she didn't escape quickly she'd be tempted to go back in and…and what? *What* was something she wasn't prepared for at the moment.

LATER THAT AFTERNOON, Tessa was on her hands and knees in the dirt, digging a hole. She sat back on her heels eyeing the depth, then glanced at the potted zinnias she planned to put there. Carefully she removed a flower from the pot, working the roots free of the plastic. After placing the plant in position she filled in the hole, gently patting the soil around the stems much like a mother soothing a fussy child.

"There now. Don't be upset. You'll like it here. You'll grow big and strong. You're an important part of this environment. Look around. This is a cottage garden, full of happy old-fashioned colorful flowers. Right behind you is cosmos. You'll be such a nice pair." She pointed to the right. "And there's larkspur and next year foxglove will bloom. You'll be happy here."

"Who are you talking to, dear?"

An elderly woman with faded blue eyes, leaning on an old-fashioned wood cane, stood just outside the door. Tessa flushed, embarrassed to be caught talking to her plants.

"I, uh…"

"Don't worry, dear, I talk to them, too. My friend Barrett told me I must speak with them every day. Do you know Barrett, Tessa? If not I'll introduce you. He's a florist and creates the most wonderful displays. He's a delightful character and has been in Warenton forever."

Tessa smiled. "I did meet him last week at a seminar. He's very talented."

"He helped me design this flower garden." Mrs. Deerfield glanced around, the love evident in her eyes. "It's been my salvation throughout my life. This is the first year I haven't been able to take care of my own garden. It's this hip, you see. I can't bend down anymore."

Tessa stood and brushed off her legs. She smiled as she took in the brilliant colors juxtaposed against the old picket fence that surrounded the garden off the back door of the weathered brick house. "It's a lovely place, Mrs. Deerfield."

"It's been in my family for a hundred and fifty years. My husband was a doctor, just like my father and grandfather. Daddy built that wing of the house for his clinic. My husband used it, too. Then he built another wing onto the house—to balance it out, he said."

"It's so peaceful out here. You're very lucky."

Mrs. Deerfield glanced at the sky.

"You need to run along. It's going to storm any minute."

Surprised, Tessa looked up, noticing the dark clouds for the first time. "I didn't realize."

With twinkling eyes, Mrs. Deerfield smiled. "You were too absorbed in your conversation, I think."

Tessa chuckled. "You're right. Well, don't worry, I can work in the rain."

"I wouldn't hear of it. My garden isn't going anywhere. You run along and have fun with your children. That's important, too."

"But—"

"No sass from you, young lady. Now, scoot!"

Tessa placed an impulsive kiss on the old lady's cheek, then obeyed. She gathered her gardening tools and containers before heading to her van. Looking at her watch, she realized it was only four o'clock. She could get some pizza and salad and have dinner with Danny and the kids.

Danny and the kids.

That sounded so homey, so like a family, that she hesitated and then decided she kind of liked it. Putting her van into gear, she drove to the nearest pizza parlor. After placing her order at the counter, she sat down to wait.

"Tessa?"

She glanced over her shoulder to see Rhonda. "Hey, Rhonda, I didn't see you when I came in."

Rhonda jerked a thumb. "I was in the bathroom freshening up. I'm meeting a guy here for dinner. If you haven't had this pizza, it's the best in the world. One bite and you'll swear you've died and gone to heaven."

Tessa smiled. Rhonda was in full exaggeration mode. Her energy for life was one of the things Tessa loved about her. "I've only been here a few times. I usually stop at a place closer to my condo."

Rhonda plopped into a chair. "Honey, if you're going to use the calories make the most of them, that's what I say."

"Thanks, Nurse Rhonda." Tessa grinned at her friend. "As usual, you've hit the nail right on the head."

"Of course I have. So how is life with the delicious Danny? That's what all of the nurses call him. They fight over who will take the emergency when we know he's on a run."

"Oh, stop it."

"I'm serious, Tessa. Many have thrown their thongs at him, but haven't scored more than a polite smile and a wicked twinkle." Rhonda nudged Tessa with her shoulder. "How are you doing in that department?"

Tessa gave Rhonda a cool look. "I'm there to babysit. I'm helping him and he's helping me. Period, end of story."

"You'd better come in to the hospital, girl. I think you need a checkup."

"Doherty," the man behind the counter called as he finished cutting the pizza. "You're up."

Tessa stood. "I'll call you later, Rhonda. Good luck with your date."

Tessa paid for the pizza and picked up the boxes. Blowing an air kiss to Rhonda, she headed for the door to drive to Danny's. As she parked in front of the house, Mrs. Deerfield's prediction came true. Rain fell in big drops onto her windshield.

Tessa managed to get the three pizza boxes, two bags and her tote bag to the porch without getting soaked. Just as she put her hip to the door to push it open, it seemed to open by itself.

"Hi, Kyle." Or was it Kevin? No, judging by the haircut it was Kyle.

"Wow, pizza." Kyle turned to shout, "Kevin, come quick."

Kevin trailed in from the living room in full Space Warrior regalia, just as Eric, nose leading the way and clutching a book about a computer program, emerged from the other side of the house. All the boys ignored Tessa, focusing on the pizza instead. *You'd think no one ever fed them.* As each of the three boys reached for a box, Tessa snatched them away.

"Wait a minute, what happened to your manners? First you say hello, and then I'll hand over the pizzas while we get ready for dinner."

The three boys looked at each other, their expressions reinforcing what they thought of this picky idea. By shared agreement they turned en masse and said, "Hi," then reached for the pizza boxes. Tessa surrendered them, calling after them, "We'll eat in the dining room. No food for you guys until I get the rest of the family in, too."

"Okay." From the angelic look on the twin's faces, Tessa expected to find a few pieces of pizza gone. She'd deal with that later. Right now she needed to fix the salad, she thought, walking toward the kitchen.

"Tessa?"

Tessa looked up at a stormy Alison leaning over the railing.

Tessa shifted the bags in her arms. "What's up, Alison? Is something wrong?"

All teenage attitude, Alison tried to stroll down the stairs, but whatever was bothering her got the better of her as she swung around the newel post in her rush to get to Tessa. "My dad is acting like a Neanderthal."

Tessa was taken aback for a moment. "He is?"

Alison nodded so hard that she resembled a bobblehead doll. "He might as well be wearing a leopard skin and carrying a club."

Tessa swallowed hard at the thought of Danny in a leopard skin. "I'm sure it's not that bad."

Alison struck a pose. "My life is ruined."

Tessa tried to hide her smile at Alison's drama-queen performance. She remembered herself at this age and wasn't looking forward to Josie behaving the same way when she was thirteen. "Why don't you help me with the salad and tell me about it?"

"Yeah, okay, I guess I could."

With Alison on her heels she entered the kitchen and unloaded her bags. Handing the lettuce to Alison, she started cutting vegetables. "All right, what is this all about, Alison?"

"Dad won't let me see my friends."

"Why not?"

Alison flung her arms wide. "Because he hates me, that's why."

This time Tessa couldn't help smiling. "Alison, your father doesn't hate you."

"Then why won't he let me go?" Alison wailed.

"Well," Tessa said in a reasonable tone, "where are you planning to go?"

"I told you, just to hang out with friends."

"That doesn't sound unreasonable."

"Tell her the rest, Alison." Danny's deep voice interrupted the conversation.

Tessa turned from making the salad to see Danny standing frozen in the doorway, his face resembling a thundercloud as he stared at his daughter. Tessa looked from one to the other and wished she could pull a vanishing act. She'd been looking forward to a casual fun evening, not being the referee in a family fight.

"Go ahead, Alison, tell Tessa all of it. Tell her where you wanted to go."

"To a club," Alison mumbled, her face set in lines of discontent.

"What kind of club?" Tessa asked.

Alison rolled her eyes as if commenting on the unreasonable behavior of the adults in her life. "A dance club. It's harmless, nothing big happening there. Just music."

Folding his arms, Danny said, "It's a weekday, Alison. You aren't allowed to go out on school nights. Those are the rules."

"It's summer, Danny. School's still out for another week or so." Tessa could have bitten her tongue for interfering as Danny's face made it very clear that her comment was unwelcome, especially when Alison jumped in to agree.

"Yeah, Dad, Tessa's right. Duh, it's still summer, remember?"

"Stow the attitude, Alison," Danny snapped. "Just because it's summer is no reason to change the rules."

Grabbing the bread sticks from the counter, Alison flounced away, but not before she got in one last zinger. "You're impossible. I wish my mother was here."

"You and me both," Danny muttered, his gaze following his daughter.

Tessa wasn't sure what to say as she glimpsed the longing in Danny's face. She wanted to take the hurt away, but didn't know how. As she opened her mouth to say something, Danny spoke instead.

He lifted his slumping shoulders, straightening to his full height. "You're back early."

Managing a smile, Tessa accepted the subject change and went back to cutting tomatoes. "It started raining and my client insisted I leave. I got pizza for dinner. The boys put it on the dining-room table."

Danny surprised Tessa with a chuckle. It was rather forced, but it was an instant mood brightener. "You left the boys alone with the pizza?"

"Yes. Dumb of me, huh?"

"I'd better rescue it before it's gone."

"Danny, would you call Josie and Emma, too? We'd better eat while we still have food left."

Danny hustled out of the kitchen, calling for the girls as he went. Tessa was given a few minutes' reprieve before she had to face Danny and Alison again. She knew Alison was counting on her support, and if she knew anything about kids Tessa knew that Alison would renew her assault after dinner, hoping to catch her father in a better mood. *Why couldn't I keep my mouth shut?* First it was her room and now dance clubs, of all things. Obviously Danny would rather she butt out, but Tessa had inserted herself into the middle of a family incident through no fault of her own. Kids were so good at playing one adult off the other that the CIA ought to recruit them as secret weapons, Tessa thought.

She sighed before picking up the salad bowl and paper plates to take into the dining room. Once there, she looked around at the table and saw the boxes open, but surprisingly no pizza gone. She sent Danny a questioning look.

Danny smiled. "It seems Eric threatened to tie the twins to a tree if they took any pizza before everyone else got here."

"Eric did that?" Tessa turned an amazed look on her son. "Who are you? What have you done with Eric the pizza hog who can't resist a piece of pizza if it's in front of him?"

Eric groaned, blushing. "Mom. Cut it out."

"Eric's a pizza hog," Josie chanted, echoed by Emma.

"All right, that's enough, young ladies," Tessa said, passing the salad around. "Alison, please pass the pepperoni pizza down here. Dig in, everyone."

Silence reigned, except for the crunch, munch, slurps and small burps from the youthful crowd around the table. Tessa glanced at Danny; he was awfully quiet. Then she remembered something and leaped up from the table. "I forgot the wine." Returning, she set the bottle of Chianti on the table in front of Danny along with two jelly jars. "I couldn't find any wineglasses."

"It doesn't matter." Danny grinned, working the corkscrew, and released the cork with a loud pop. "These will work." He poured the wine and toasted Tessa, "Cheers."

"Cheers."

"Can we go now, Mom? We're done," Eric said, with a look around the table.

"Okay, take your plates into the kitchen, scrape them and throw them in the recycle can." One by one the children left the table, with the last to leave being Alison, who gave her father a pathetic look as she went past.

"Dad…"

"I don't want to talk about it, Alison."

Tessa toyed with her wine as Alison left the room, her feet dragging like a woman on her way to the executioner's block. "Danny, I don't mean to interfere, but don't you think you're being a bit unfair?"

Danny turned a cold face to her. "Unfair? No, I don't think so. I don't want my barely-fourteen-year-old daughter out at a dance club with God knows whom. Anything could happen to her."

"I didn't mean that. I meant by not speaking to her and letting her make her case."

"I did speak to her."

"To her or at her?"

With a scowl, Danny looked down at his wine. "I don't know what that means. We have rules. Alison knows that. The rules guarantee a safer life."

"Surely you can bend them a bit now and then?"

"Look, I've been father and mother to these kids for the past three years. That's the long and short of it. I'm doing what my wife would approve, even though you don't." With a challenging look at Tessa, he refilled their jars.

"All I'm suggesting is you talk rationally and explain your reasons."

Danny took a big gulp of his drink. "My reasons are very simple. I said no. Don't tell me you're one of those women who let their kids run over them."

"No, I believe in reasonable limits and communicating with my children."

"Did your husband feel that way, too?"

"Not exactly. When he noticed the kids at all, he was much like you in some ways. He was always convinced he was right. He made the money, so he made the rules, he said." Tessa drained her glass. "One day he made one rule too many and that was that."

Refilling their glasses again, Danny said, "My wife liked having someone helping to make decisions. We were a team."

"A team where you made most of the rules, though. Right, Danny?"

"We didn't think of our relationship that way—not after I started my career with the fire department. It just made sense and made our family life easier to handle. After she died, I guess our family rules became more important to me."

"You must miss her very much."

"Yes, I do, especially now that Alison is growing up. She looks so much like her mother. I just want to protect her and keep her safe the way I couldn't with Laurie."

"I know, Danny. I wasn't criticizing. But girls are so different than boys."

Danny exhaled. "That's the truth."

"When my mother could bother to notice me, she'd tell me that if I didn't shape up she'd trade me in for a new model."

Laughing, but with a touch of sympathy in his eyes, Danny

touched his glass to Tessa's. "I'll keep that in mind." His gaze met hers, the sudden warmth in it bringing a flush to Tessa's cheeks. He reached out and touched her nose. "Your nose is pink. Is it too hot in here? I can turn on the fan."

"Just call me Rudolph," Tessa quipped, flushing even more. "I always get a red nose when I drink wine." *And when you look at me like that and touch me I get even more flustered.*

"Well, it's a good thing it's gone then, isn't it?"

Horrified, Tessa peered at the wine bottle. "We drank the whole bottle!"

Danny's laughed boomed. "You make it sound as if we were having an orgy. The whole bottle is only three glasses each."

Tessa spoke without thinking. "I thought an orgy meant sex and food. Don't you need those, too?"

Eyes gleaming, Danny stared at her over his wine. "Is that an offer?"

"What? Oh, no, no, of course not."

"I wasn't sure, because we've already had the food, so I thought—"

"You did not."

Danny raised an eyebrow. "I'll tell you what. I'll make some coffee and we can talk it over."

"Why don't you plug in the coffeemaker and then go talk to Alison?"

Danny stood and picked up the bottle and glasses. "You're not going to let that drop, are you?"

"I think you'll both feel better. Maybe she can invite some friends over instead." Tessa grinned. "It's always good to have a counter offer in your pocket."

"I'll try to remember that." He went to the kitchen to start the coffee.

Tessa propped her chin on one hand and fanned herself with the other in an attempt to cool down—from the wine or the conversation, she wasn't sure which. After a few minutes she was fighting to keep her eyes open. After all the fresh air, working the dirt, a full stomach and three glasses of wine, she'd give anything to curl up and take a nap. Yawning, she stood and stretched. She noticed the window seat in the dining room's bay window, now shaded by the big oak trees outside. She'd been wanting to try it out.

When Danny came back with the coffee, he discovered Tessa sound asleep. Quietly he put the coffee down and walked over to look at her. She looked exhausted. Her hands were folded like a child at prayer, curling tendrils of hair framed her face, long eyelashes brushed pink cheeks and her pursed lips made a charming sound, almost like a gurgle, although he'd tell her she snored when she woke up later. There was something about teasing her that was just irresistible.

He decided to let her sleep for a while and took the kids out for some ice cream. When he got them back to the house he settled them down with a DVD and went in to check on Tessa. Since she was still asleep, he got his training manuals and began to study for an advanced fire qualification. Except for the sound of the TV in the living room, the house was quiet, peaceful. Another half hour passed before Tessa stirred. Danny took off his glasses and watched her wake, her movements bringing an ache to his heart. How many times had he found Laurie grabbing a quick nap in that very spot? Too many to remember. And now Tessa was doing the same thing. She looked nothing like Laurie, not really, but every once in a while there was an expression and an attitude that reminded him of what he'd lost.

Tessa pulled him from his melancholy thoughts as she jerked to a sitting position. "Oh…what time is it?"

Danny glanced at his watch. "Just after eight."

"I fell asleep, didn't I?"

With a chuckle, Danny studied her dismayed face. "Either that or you were in a hypnotic trance for the past hour and a half."

"Where are the kids?"

"I stuffed them full of ice cream and put them in front of the boob tube."

"I'm so sorry. I didn't mean to leave you on child-care duty tonight."

"No problem. I think you needed the sleep."

"I haven't been sleeping well."

"Anything I can do to help?" He didn't mean that to come out seductively, but it did.

"Such as?" Tessa asked with a mistrustful glance.

He laughed. "Shame on you if you're thinking what I think you're thinking."

Tessa laughed back, acknowledging the hit. "I'm not awake yet." She yawned. "I have to round up the kids and get home. I have some things to do tonight."

"Why don't you stay? I have to work tomorrow, so you have to come back anyway."

Tessa looked at him, a long look that started his blood boiling. "I don't think that's a good idea."

"Why not? You spend the night when I'm not here."

"Exactly. That's the point—you're not here." Standing, Tessa smoothed her hair and tucked in her shirt before she looked at him again. "I just think it would be better if I go home."

Danny nodded. "Whatever you say. You're the boss."

"Oh, now I'm the boss."

He smiled. "At the moment."

"I guess that's better than nothing." She turned to smooth the pillows on the window seat.

"I talked to Alison."

That statement got her full attention. "You did? What happened?"

"Nothing much, but at least we're talking. I told her she could plan next week for some friends to come over. After I meet them, then we can discuss her going out sometimes with these friends."

"Great. That's just great, Danny."

Danny shrugged. "I hope so, because my every instinct is to lock my little girl in a tower and throw away the key."

"I'm sure most fathers feel like that."

"Wait until Josie is fourteen. Your ex-husband will be a nervous wreck."

"I doubt that. He's too busy finding female friends of his own to worry about Josie."

"He what?"

"I'll see you tomorrow morning," Tessa added, walking from the room to leave Danny to wonder just what had made Tessa divorce her husband after all—her desire for independence or his infidelity.

Chapter Six

A few days later, on Sunday morning, Danny woke up early. He wandered down to the kitchen and made a cup of extra-strong coffee. He stretched his aching muscles, realizing he'd spent too much time Saturday working on the boat he was restoring. The house was silent around him. His children were still asleep, but instead of the usual reassuring feeling, the silence made Danny restless.

Carrying his mug to the front porch, he bent to retrieve the paper. More than anything else, Danny missed the Sunday mornings spent with his wife. When his off days fell on a Sunday they'd wake early, he'd lock the door and then he and Laurie would snuggle in bed, whispering, touching and giggling like children before following up the touching and laughter with lovemaking.

Danny sighed, then sipped his coffee before placing it on the table to attack the paper. More bad news. Suddenly restless, he tossed the paper aside. Grabbing his coffee mug, he stalked across the porch and leaned against the railing. It was going to be a warm day judging by the sky and the early-morning sun that peeked shyly around a cloud. It was a day made for—for what? Danny's restlessness increased as he decided it was a day for something special, something magical.

He wondered what Tessa was doing today.

He sipped his coffee and hitched a leg up to sit on the rail. Maybe he should call her. He could just say hello, hi, how ya' doing, and then suggest they do something…with the kids, of course. It would be just a casual outing, no big deal. It wouldn't be because he wanted to see her. It would be a change of pace, with both of them and all of the kids together doing something.

Without giving himself time to change his mind, he flipped his cell phone out of his jeans pocket and dialed Tessa's number. It rang for what seemed a long time, but just as he was about to hang up he heard Tessa answer.

"Hello." Her voice was husky with sleep.

"Tessa?"

"Mmm-hmm," she purred, causing Danny to grip the phone as all his muscles tightened in response.

"Tessa, it's Danny."

"Mmm-hmm," she repeated, sounding all cozy and only half-awake.

"Tessa, are you awake?"

"Awake?" she repeated, obviously still half-asleep.

He chuckled at her incoherence. "Yes, awake. It's Danny."

"Danny." She sighed. Then her voice sharpened. "Danny, what's wrong?"

"Nothing's wrong. Everything's fine."

"What time is it?"

"I don't know. Early." He checked his watch. "Oops, very early."

"It's five forty-five! It's Sunday. You have the day off. I have the day off. I like to sleep late on my day off."

He winced at her tone. "Would you like me to call you back later?"

"Yes. No. I'm awake now."

"I was thinking," Danny said, Rubbing the back of his neck. "You have the day free, I have the day free—let's do something together."

"Together," she said slowly, "as in you and me?"

"Well, you, me and six kids."

"What did you have in mind?"

"I wasn't sure. Maybe canoeing and a picnic. How does that sound?"

"Like hard work. I've only been canoeing once since I was a kid."

"Don't worry, it'll come back to you." Danny played his trump card. "Your kids will love it."

"I'm not sure it's a good…" She was silent for a moment and Danny could swear he heard the wheels turning. Finally Tessa said, "Okay, okay, we'll go."

"Great, I'll pack a picnic lunch and—"

"I'll pack the lunch," she said, obviously gaining her full senses by the minute. "I'm not as fond of peanut butter as you are and that's all you seem to eat."

"That's un-American. Next thing is you hate apple pie."

"Not true. I love apple pie." Tessa exhaled, now sounding wide-awake and laughing. "How do you always suck me into these idiotic conversations?"

Danny laughed back. "I'll pick you up at nine, okay?"

"Fine. See you then."

At nine o'clock on the dot, Danny knocked on Tessa's door, leaving three excited kids bouncing in his SUV. As usual, Alison was pouting in a corner very unhappy that Tessa was coming with them. Or as she had put it, "We don't need her along." Danny hoped the day would go smoothly without one of Ali's famous sulkfests. Maybe he should have let her bring a friend, as she'd asked. But he wanted this day to be about their families having fun together.

He knocked again and this time the door opened immediately. He was almost barreled over by Josie and Eric as they ran to the car, leaving Tessa standing there with a tote bag and huge straw picnic basket. Danny ran a quick eye over her, from her feet in canvas boat shoes up her long legs to stylish shorts and a coordinating top to the floppy straw hat perched on her head. She looked as if she was headed for a day sailing on a yacht instead of a day on the river in a canoe. He'd have to take her out on his sailboat if he ever completed his renovations.

Tessa frowned. "Why are you staring at me?"

Danny met her eyes. She looked a bit defensive as well as wary, as if she was doing something incorrectly. As he stared at her, something vulnerable came into her eyes and she touched her hat. "Did I do something wrong?"

"No," Danny said, his tone gentle. "You look lovely. I like the hat—it will keep the sun off this cute little nose." He couldn't resist touching the nose in question. He wanted to take her in his arms and soothe her sudden anxiety, but he didn't think she'd appreciate it.

"Let's go, you guys," one of the kids yelled.

Danny laughed. "Ah, the sweet voices of our children's bellow. Here, let me take the basket." He took it from her and led the way to the car. "This is heavy. You must have packed for an army."

"I packed extra for this bunch."

A half hour later they arrived at the canoe rental, rented canoes and were ready to hit the water.

"How are we going to do this?" Tessa asked, a worried look on her face. "There are two canoes, but the kids and I are practically novices, so I don't think—"

"Don't worry. I'll take Emma, Josie and Kyle. You'll take Alison, Eric and Kevin."

"But—" Tessa said, about to protest.

"Dad, I don't want to go with her. I want to go with you," Alison wailed. At her father's look she flushed as she realized how rude she had been. "I don't mean I don't want to go with you, Tessa. I just haven't been canoeing with Dad for a long time is all. We used to do it more often when my mother…"

"It's okay, Alison, I understand.'

Danny glanced at Tessa and saw that she probably did understand very well. "No, Ali," he said, his impatience with Alison's attitude breaking through. "You're going in Tessa's canoe and I don't want to hear anything else about it." Danny turned to Tessa.

"There's nothing to worry about," he said, handing Tessa a paddle. "It will all come back to you. Besides, Alison and Kevin are old hands on the river and Eric will catch on with no problem. Just remember to use the paddle on both sides of the canoe and develop your rhythm. That's it. "

"It will be a piece of cake, I suppose?" Tessa murmured with a pointed look at Danny, who only grinned.

Eric patted his mother's arm. "Don't worry, Mom. If you fall overboard, we'll haul you out."

"Great. Thanks, Eric," Tessa said with a skeptical look at the canoe. Then Danny saw her glance at Alison, probably wondering if the teenager would do the same.

Emma walked over to Tessa and patted her leg. "Don't worry, Tessa. Daddy won't let anything happen to you, 'cause he's a fireman and he rescues people."

Tessa knelt to give the little girl a big hug. "Thanks, Emma. I feel better now."

Emma grinned, then whispered in Tessa's ear, her breath tickling. "But you have to be good or he won't let you ride his big boat when he gets it finished."

"Okay," Tessa whispered back.

Then Danny struck a pose resembling a general addressing his troops. "We're burning daylight, people. Now, once in the water, I'll take the lead. Make sure you all wear your life jackets. Oh, and don't stand up. Emma, come on, you're with me."

With a determined grip, Tessa stalked over to the first canoe. "All right, Eric, grab the picnic basket and let's go." Danny and the kids followed, and without mishap they pushed off into the river.

Tessa's canoe was a bit unsteady and tended to go in circles every once in a while, but for the most part both teams survived without trauma, except for Emma losing a barrette when she bent over to peer into the water at a fish.

"That's where we'll stop," Danny called, pointing at a small area surrounded by forest. Both canoe teams headed toward shore.

Arms and legs aching with effort and tension, Tessa managed to haul herself out of the canoe without falling flat on her face. She was tempted to kiss the ground at having made it downstream successfully.

Danny slung a friendly arm around her shoulders. "How are you doing?"

"If my muscles would quit shaking I could tell you."

Laughing, Danny squeezed her. "Don't worry, you'll get used to it. You're using different muscles than you usually do."

"Trust me, I'm using muscles I didn't know existed." Looking around, she stepped away from Danny. "Where are the picnic tables?"

"There aren't any. This isn't a developed picnic area, but at the other edge of the woods is a small clearing that will be perfect for sitting on the ground."

"I have a blanket, so we can spread that."

"That's what I love—a woman who thinks of everything."

Tessa could feel her cheeks flush at Danny's comment. Love? *Stop imagining things. He didn't mean it that way.* Trying to ignore her quickening pulse, she changed the subject, "Okay, lead on. The kids are probably starving."

"Let's go, gang," Danny said, picking up the tote bag and picnic basket and heading into the forest with Josie, Emma and the twins whooping and hollering behind him. Not wanting to be stuck with the women, Eric hustled to catch up with Danny, while Tessa and Alison brought up the rear.

"Thanks for helping paddle, Alison. I couldn't have done it without you. You were a lifesaver."

Alison gave her a typical shrug and muttered, "No big deal."

"Yes, it was. I'd still be circling in the water if it weren't for you. So thanks." Tessa nudged Alison with her elbow, trying to get a response.

"Everyone does that at first."

"Do they? I'll bet your mom was good at it," Tessa said, hoping the young girl would warm up and talk about her mother.

Alison hesitated, then confessed, "My mom was hopeless."

Tessa smiled. "I don't believe that. You're just trying to make me feel better. From the way your dad talks, your mother did everything very well."

"She did, but I think she was afraid of the water. She only went because Dad and us kids liked to go." Alison's face clouded with memories. "Mom was brave like that."

"She sounds wonderful. I wish I'd known her. You must really miss her." Tessa's compassion rushed over her, but she resisted touching Alison to comfort her, as she wasn't sure it would be welcome.

Alison nodded. "She always made time to talk to me. I could tell her stuff and she understood."

Tessa adjusted her hat as a beam of sunlight spiked through the trees. "You were very lucky to have her, Alison. I couldn't do that with my mother. She was always too busy with my dad, the house, or her committees, things like that."

Tessa felt as if she was a bug under a microscope as Alison considered her comment. "That's weird. Didn't she love you?"

"Oh yes, but…" Tessa wrinkled her nose, not sure how to express her thoughts. "I think she was reserved and afraid to show too much emotion, especially to her only girl. I don't know why. She was older when I was born, so maybe that had something to do with it. Times and attitudes were changing for women, but she was trying to raise me as if they weren't."

"My mom wouldn't have done that. She was cool," Alison pointed out, almost choking on the last word.

Tessa stopped and risked placing her hand on Alison's arm. "Alison, if something is bothering you and you want to talk, you can talk to me." At Alison's solemn look, she rushed on. "I know I'm not your mother, but I understand how hard it is to be your age. Sometimes one woman needs to talk to another." Tessa smiled as Alison seemed to fight against accepting anything from Tessa but eventually puffed with pride because she'd been called a woman. Without waiting for a response, Tessa said, "We'd better catch up with the others before the twins eat all the food. I'm surprised the picnic basket survived the trip in one piece."

"That's because Dad was protecting it."

"Then he's our hero," Tessa breathed in a rescued-heroine voice.

Alison laughed, a free joyous laugh that transformed her face into a young woman on the threshold of life. It was such a change from her normal sulky pout that Tessa blinked away a sudden tear, unable to say anything for a moment. She was tempted to comment on Ali's lovely smile, but was afraid it would disappear if she did so. Tessa cleared her throat, finally saying, "Let's get going." They set off, finding Danny and the kids in the promised clearing a short way ahead.

"Hey there, slowpokes," Danny said with a welcoming grin. "We thought we'd lost you."

"You wish," Alison teased, her good mood still holding. Her father rewarded her humor by gently tugging on her hair.

"We don't need Alison, Dad. She's just a girl," the twins yelled before grabbing Eric and dashing into the forest, with Alison and the rest of the girls accepting the challenge and taking off in hot pursuit.

"If we're lucky," Danny said in a mock stage whisper, "they won't come back and we can gorge ourselves on lunch."

Tessa laughed. "Keep dreaming, fireman. The minute those boys smell food, they'll trample us to get to it." She knelt to rummage in the tote bag. Extracting a blanket, she spread it on the ground before unpacking the picnic basket.

Danny knelt with her. "Let me help." Together they set out the food, Danny sneaking a taste from the covered dishes as he did so. "This pasta salad is great. I like all the vegetables you added."

"I have to sneak them in so the kids eat them without complaining."

"Well, this sure is better than peas in the macaroni," Danny said, taking another mouthful. "I'll call the monsters."

Laughing, Tessa pointed at the woods. "No need, here they come. I told you they'd smell the food."

One by one the kids trailed out of the woods. Upon spying the lunch they descended like locusts and proceeded to devour the turkey sandwiches, pasta salad, pickles, chips and lemonade. It took some effort, but Tessa and Danny finally managed to snag their own food. Tessa looked around at the happy kids before she caught Danny's gaze. She blushed at the warmth in his eyes as he shared the moment with her. She started to say something, but wasn't sure what to say, and Danny smiled. Luckily for Tessa, Eric interrupted, especially since Alison was watching them.

"What's for dessert, Mom?" Eric asked.

It took a moment for Tessa to pull herself together and throw out a teasing "What makes you think I brought dessert?"

"Because you always bring dessert."

Danny looked only a bit less expectant than the kids. "You brought dessert? What kind?"

Tessa pulled a covered plate from the bottom of the basket. With a flourish she removed the cover. "Great big homemade double-chocolate chip cookies."

"Wow, you're the best mom in the whole wide world," Josie yelled, reaching for a cookie.

"Don't grab, kids—there's enough for everyone." Tessa grinned and slapped Danny's hand as he reached for a second cookie. "Greedy."

Danny's expression changed from sexy tough male to that of a deprived child. "Did I ever tell you how much I love chocolate-chip cookies? How I haven't had homemade ones forever?"

Alison called him on the statement. "Dad, that isn't true. I made some last week."

"Honey, you can't compare chocolate-chip cookies you slice off a roll and bake to these masterpieces."

Alison stared at her father, the struggle over going along with the teasing or getting angry at a perceived slight obvious on her face, so Tessa jumped in to change the subject. "Everyone, put your plates and cups into the garbage bag." Watching as the kids obeyed, she asked, "What were you kids doing in the woods before? Exploring?"

"We're warriors and we're hunting because we're hungry and we have to feed the tribe," Kevin piped up.

"We can't find any food, so we're going to attack the fort," Kyle finished in a bloodthirsty manner.

"Who is in the fort?" Danny asked, idly licking chocolate off his fingers.

Kevin gave him an incredulous look. "The girls, of course."

Danny nodded. "Right. I should have guessed that."

Josie stood and brushed the crumbs from her shorts. "But we aren't going to let them win. Are we, girls?" Emma shook her head so hard that her ponytail bounced in a circle.

"Nope. Let's go," Alison said, dropping back into childhood as she raced into the woods with the two younger girls right behind her. The boys stayed only to grab another cookie before they took off in pursuit.

Danny cleaned up the rest of the mess while Tessa repacked the picnic basket. After watching Tessa fussing around for a few more minutes, he grabbed her arm and pulled her gently down to sit on the blanket next to him. "Relax. It's Sunday and my only Sunday off in quite a while."

"Do you like being a firefighter?"

"I never wanted to do anything else."

"All little boys want to be a fireman when they grow up, don't they?"

Danny chuckled. "Well, they sure do if they come from a family of firefighters."

"Did you?"

"Yes, my dad and before that my grandpa."

"Here in Warenton?"

"That's right. They weren't located in the same firehouse, but they were in the department. Grandpa died a few years ago." Danny's face grew taut with memory. "Dad died in a fire. A beam fell when he was rescuing a woman who'd been trapped in the bedroom. She made it, he didn't."

Tessa touched his arm. "I'm so sorry, Danny. Is your

mother—" Tessa stopped, not able to go on, afraid of bringing up too many unhappy memories.

"Mom was here for a while, but it was hard for her. Finally she decided to move to Missouri to live with her sister, who was also widowed. They live on a horse farm a couple hours from St. Louis. The kids and I visit when we can, and she comes up here to see them." He leaned back on his elbow, propping his head on his hand. "How about you? Tell me about your family. Do they live in the area?"

Tessa shifted, clasping her arms around her raised knees. "No. They're in San Francisco now. Dad's a corporate executive. Mom is the perfect corporate wife. We lived in Chicago when I was in school. Right after I went away to college, Dad was promoted again into a position that included a lot of travel, and they move every three years."

"Did your husband work for the same company?"

"Ex-husband," Tessa corrected, her tone brittle. "Yes, that's where I met him. Dad introduced us. Colin was the up-and-coming young exec, so Dad thought he'd be suitable for his only daughter."

"But he wasn't?" Danny asked, a gentle look on his face.

"He was for a while. We were happy. He worked and I helped him move up the ladder. To our friends we were the perfect couple. I got pregnant with Eric. Thank goodness he was a boy. That's what Colin wanted, a little Mini-Me. Then Josie came along, and by then Colin was scarcely home. At least, he wasn't home in our house. It turns out he was at home in other women's houses."

"Is that why you divorced him?"

"Not completely," Tessa said, drawing out the words as she shook her head. "As the kids got older I wanted something else. I wanted to accomplish more than just throw successful parties for Colin's clients and hang out with suitable wives who bored me to death. I wanted to use my college degree for something more than just arranging flowers. I told Colin I wanted to start a business."

"How did he take it?"

"How do you think? He told me it would take too much time away from him. He wanted me at home. That was the beginning of the end, I guess."

"Well, I can see his point in a way. About staying home, I mean."

Affronted, Tessa turned to face Danny. "What do you mean?"

Danny sat up. "Well, the guy had a pretty intense career and he needed your help."

Pointing at her chest, Tessa said, "What about my needs? I needed something, too."

"Sure, I know. I only meant that maybe he had a good reas—"

"What about the affairs?" Tessa demanded. "I suppose he had a good reason for that, too. Like maybe I'm not pretty enough, or sexy enough, or…"

Danny reached a hand to cup her neck. "Now, hold on. I said nothing about the affairs. I was only pointing out that—"

"Stop pointing," Tessa said, pushing his hand away. "You know nothing about my life. I'm surprised you didn't say he should have chained me to the kitchen stove. That's probably what you did with your wife."

Cupping her shoulders, Danny said, "Hold on, there. I didn't make her do anything like that. Laurie was home because she wanted to be home. But I'm glad she was. That's the type of person a man like me needs."

"Because you're a firefighter?" Tessa rolled her eyes, "Oh please. I'm sure there are women with careers married to firemen."

Danny released her. "No, that's not why…well, not

entirely… We had four kids. She wanted to be home with them. I was proud and happy that she wanted that life. She might have gotten a job sometime later when the kids were older, but meanwhile I—"

"Kept her chained to the stove, chained to the cribs and chained to the bed so she'd be available when you wanted her, I'll bet."

Danny laughed. "No, only chained to the bed."

Tessa leaped to her feet and grabbed the edge of the blanket. Tugging, she attempted to dislodge Danny. "Get up. It's time to go."

Grinning, Danny lay back and folded his arms under his head, the picture of confident amused male. "Make me."

Tessa tugged again, but couldn't move him. Infuriated by the conversation, she dropped to her knees and attempted to roll him off the blanket. It was like trying to move a boulder. "I said get up."

With a chuckle, Danny just lay there, an immovable object. Tessa didn't quit, though. With a mighty shove she moved him a bit, but lost her balance and fell on his chest. Promptly his arms came around her.

"Who said you weren't sexy? Your husband must have been an idiot."

Tessa struggled to get up, but Danny just laughed and held on. "Will you let me go!"

"Nope."

"I'm your sitter, for heaven's sake."

Danny winked. "You're not *my* sitter."

"You know what I mean." Placing her hands on his chest, Tessa reared back to look him in the face. Her anger faltered as she saw his smiling expression. Then she saw the look in his eyes change from playfulness to something warmer, something that caused her breath to catch in her throat.

"Danny," Tessa whispered. "Danny, what are you doing?"

"I don't know," Danny replied, his voice slow and deep. "All I know is I've wanted to hold you like this since you knocked on my door that first day looking as if you were afraid I'd bite."

"Danny, we can't do this."

"Tessa, we aren't doing anything. Yet," he added.

"We can't get involved. We have too much baggage."

Danny shifted so he could cup her face with his hands. "So we can unpack." Without either of them considering it further, they flowed together like a slowly moving creek. Their lips met tentatively at first, then as they became more comfortable, more firmly. It was a kiss of comfort, of friendliness, of companionship. Tessa wasn't sure when it changed. Their lips became more intense, but they both froze when they heard one of the kids yell.

"Hey, Mom, come see what we found," Eric called.

Tessa took advantage of Danny's loosened arms and jerked away. She struggled to sit up, but had problems because her arm was trapped under his body and her thin gold bracelet was tangled with one of Danny's shirt buttons. "Oh, for—"

Danny sat up, with Tessa still attached. With a sideways glance at the forest she pulled harder to untangle them. "Don't yank on it like that—you'll break the chain. Let me help."

"Oh, you've helped, all right. What were you thinking, kissing me?"

"I wasn't thinking."

"That much is obvious."

"I didn't notice you complaining."

"I—" Tessa stopped. "You took me by surprise."

"No, I didn't. You could have stopped me. All you had to do was say no."

Biting her lip, Tessa said, "Okay, you're right. Maybe I didn't want to say no."

"I know," Danny said, stroking her cheek. "I didn't want you to."

"Mom," Eric yelled again, running out of the woods toward the blanket with the twins and Alison behind him. "You have to come quick. There's this kitten and he's—" Eric stopped as if he'd been shot. "What are you doing?"

His question was echoed by Alison's shocked gasp and a terse question of her own. "Dad, what's going on here?"

Danny held up his hand. "It's not what you think, honey."

Unwilling to look up at the kids, Tessa echoed his denial. "No, it's not. My bracelet got caught in Danny's shirt button when I was trying to get him off the blanket." She prayed her hair wasn't as messy as she thought it might be from the suspicious look Alison cast her way.

"Uh-huh," Alison said in that noncommittal way that meant *I don't believe a word of it.* So much for the progress Tessa thought she was making with the girl.

Not looking at Tessa either, Danny laughed, trying to play off the awkward situation. "That'll teach me to try to steal some cookies. Tessa shoved me away and her bracelet got caught."

"Mom?" Eric shifted his attention back to his mother.

"He's right. I was trying to save some cookies for you guys so Danny didn't eat them all."

Two suspicious faces and the mischievous faces of the twins looked them over. At those looks Tessa yanked her arm away, breaking her bracelet, which tumbled onto the blanket.

"Ah, Tessa, look what you did. You broke it."

"It doesn't matter," Tessa said as she scrambled to her feet. It did, though. She'd been given that thin gold ID chain when she graduated from high school. As much as she regretted breaking it, she regretted the expression on the children's faces more.

Danny picked up the bracelet, tucking it into his pocket before walking over to the kids. "What's all this about a kitten?"

"He's stuck, Dad," Kyle said.

"He needs help." Kevin agreed.

Danny flexed his muscles like a strongman. "Then you came to the right place. Big tough fireman to the rescue." He glanced back at Tessa. "You coming?"

Tessa wasted no time joining them, asking Eric, "Is the kitten hurt?"

"We don't know, Mom. We can't get him out of the hole to see."

"Let's go, then."

The kids led the way following a path in the wood, veering off at a slight hill that descended into a patch of blackberry bushes with Josie and Emma sitting still as little mice beside it, peering into the brambles.

"He's down there," Alison said, pointing to the bushes.

Danny paused. "He's tangled in the thorns, you mean? I thought you said he was in a hole."

"He is. There's a hole in the ground in the middle of the bushes. Maybe an animal dug a den or something."

Tessa was right behind a muttering Danny as he scrambled down the hill, where he received an enthusiastic hug from Emma and another from Josie. To the children he was the big strong hero to the rescue, and if she was truthful with herself—to her, too.

"He's right in there, Daddy. You can see his eyes."

"He's all scared, Danny," Josie wailed, holding Danny's arm, releasing it only after he patted her hand.

"Don't worry." Danny grabbed a dead branch, then moved to the bushes. "All right, you guys, all of you stay out of the way and don't try to follow me. I'll get him out if I can."

"You hast to, Daddy," Emma begged. "He's lonely and crying. He can't find his mommy, either."

Tessa knelt to gather Emma and Josie into her arms. "Don't you worry, darling, your daddy will get him out."

"My daddy can do anything. Can't you, Daddy?"

With a sheepish grin, Danny had no choice but to nod. He pretended to push back his sleeves. "Stand back and marvel. The fireman is on the job." Using the branch as a machete, he pushed the blackberry stems aside as he stepped into the tangled branches.

Tessa winced as the thorns caught on Danny's shirt and tore at his skin. At one violent exclamation, Tessa said, "Cover your ears, kids." As Danny pushed farther into the thicket, a moment of silence ensued. Tessa peered into the bushes. "Danny, are you okay?"

"I'm okay. I found him."

"Can you get him out?"

"He's slipped down pretty far, but I think so." Another long moment passed with the kids all shifting and shuffling their feet as they waited. Finally they heard a pathetic meow.

"Got him," Danny called. "Ow, get your claws out of me, Fuzzface." Danny emerged from the brambles, his shirt torn, his arms and face scratched and bleeding and with a pathetic kitten holding on to him for dear life. "Here he is."

The excited kids all reached for the kitten, but Tessa got to him first. "Ah, the poor little guy."

"Yeah, the poor little guy has claws the size of a grizzly bear."

Tessa cuddled him close. "Oh, Danny, don't exaggerate. He's so thin. He must have been out here a long time."

"Can we keep him, Mom?" Josie asked. "You said we could have a pet someday."

"Well, I don't know. I'm not sure we can have pets in our condo."

Eric added his *please* to Josie's. "He won't take up much room, Mom. No one will know."

Tessa cast a pleading glance at Danny. "Danny, you were the hero. Maybe you would…"

Danny backed up, hands in the air. "No, thanks. I've got a dog."

"And the baby squirrel Kyle and me found," Kevin added.

Danny sent Kevin a quizzical look. "What baby squirrel? Oh, never mind…and a squirrel. I don't need anything more."

"Your house is so much big—"

"You can bring him over to visit," Danny said, folding his arms.

"Thanks a heap," Tessa said with a wry grimace.

"Can we, Mom? Can we keep him? We can call him Fuzzface like Danny said."

Tessa gave in. "Okay, fine, but the two of you have to take care of him—or is it a her? A 'her' can have kittens."

"It's a him. Hims just get to make kittens," Danny said with a look that Tessa tried to ignore.

Eric took the kitten from Tessa. "We'll take good care of him, Mom. Come on, let's go home so we can get him some food. I'll bet he's hungry."

"Maybe there's something left from lunch," Alison said, leading the way back to the picnic site with Eric and Emma right behind her.

"We might have cookies left," Kyle said, racing ahead with his twin right behind him.

"Kitties can't have cookies," Josie said. "Can they, Mommy?"

"No, they can't." Tessa slapped at a bite on her arm before calling after Josie, who was rushing to catch up with the others. "Josie, tell Eric that kitten needs a bath, too."

Danny nodded. "He really stinks."

"I noticed." For the first time since he'd brought the kitten out, Tessa took a really good look at Danny. "Oh my God, you're a mess. You're bleeding."

"They're just scratches from the thorns. It's fine."

"No, it isn't fine. They could get infected. We have to wash and disinfect those right away."

Danny slung his arm around her shoulders. "That sounds promising. I have a big shower stall."

Tessa slapped at his hand and shrugged his arm away. "Stop that."

"Sorry."

Looking up into Danny's twinkling eyes, Tessa couldn't help but smile back. "You are not."

"You caught me."

"Let's go home."

"You got it, lady. Maybe I can change your mind about that shower."

"Look, Danny. What happened before…well, it was…" She stumbled over a tree root and would have fallen if Danny hadn't taken her arm. She could feel his hand burning her flesh. She had to get herself under control. Danny Santori was way too attractive for her peace of mind. The best thing she could do was keep her distance from him and not let herself think of that kiss again.

Danny caressed her arm. "Was enjoyable, you were starting to say?"

"No. Yes, I mean, it was. But it can't happen again."

"Why not? I'm single, you're single."

"We have a professional arrangement, that's why. I don't want to screw it up."

"I don't, either, but you can't deny that there's something between us. I don't see why we can't enjoy it."

"It might get messy, that's why."

Danny stopped and gently turned Tessa to face him. "Tessa, life is messy."

"Don't patronize me. I know very well how messy life is. But I can't afford to split my focus between what I'm trying to accomplish and a romance. I have too much riding on making a success of my life now to fall for a sexy fireman who needs a diversion."

"A diversion. That's what you think this is about?"

"It can't be about anything else. I'm not the type of woman you want."

"You could be."

"And pigs can fly," Tessa quipped, thinking he was joking with her. Then, glimpsing his serious and determined expression, she sobered. "No. I couldn't, Danny. I admire women who are completely fulfilled with their marriage and all, but I don't want to be one of them. I've already tried it and it didn't work very well the first time."

"Maybe your husband wasn't the right man."

"He wasn't. But to be fair, I probably wasn't the right woman for him, either. He needed someone who would always take a backseat, not complain about anything and ignore his affairs. I could only do that for so long."

"People can change if they want to, Tessa."

"That's the point, Danny. I did. He didn't," she said, her gaze as serious and determined now as his as she stepped toward him. "Look, I've taken a huge chance moving here and starting a business. I can't risk getting personally involved, regardless of how tempting it is."

His mouth grim, Danny stared at her for a long moment. "Well, that's clear enough."

"I'm sorry. But I'm sure you won't have any trouble finding another—"

"Diversion?" he asked. "Don't worry about me. I'm not

so hard up that I have to push myself on someone who doesn't want me."

At his harsh tone, Tessa winced as if he'd struck her. "Danny," she said, reaching out to him, "I didn't mean to hurt your feelings."

Danny backed up to avoid her touch. He gave her a bright brittle smile. "Don't give yourself so much credit."

Tessa didn't know what to say.

"Come on," Danny said, "let's get back. I'm on call later and I'd like to get closer to home in case I'm needed." He stalked out of the woods, grabbing the picnic basket as he passed. Silently Tessa picked up the blanket, hugging it to her as she followed him to the canoes.

Chapter Seven

A few days later Danny was in the firehouse garage, still brooding over the incident with Tessa. He didn't understand the woman. It wasn't as if he was proposing or anything. *It was just a kiss,* he thought, *a kiss that had a lot of promise, but still just a kiss. Why did she have to make such a big deal about it?*

"Women!"

"What's that? Did you say something, Danny?" CJ Doren asked as she walked over to where he stood checking the equipment on the fire truck.

Danny glanced at the tall attractive woman. "I said women."

"I heard that part. What I didn't hear was why."

"You're a woman, CJ...."

"Yeah, so?"

"So, okay, here goes... Can a woman say she wants something but not know that what she wants is something else?"

"Oh boy, this is going to be one of those discussions, isn't it?" Obviously stalling, CJ pulled off her firehouse baseball hat to readjust her ponytail. "Are you referring to anyone in particular? Or is it a general question?"

"Never mind," Danny said. "Forget I asked."

"Okay. Listen, I came to tell you that the chief wants to see you. Maybe you should ask him."

"Mike Crezinski isn't a woman."

CJ rolled her eyes. "Well, jeez, no kidding, Sherlock. I said that because he's been involved with more women than you have, and so has Jake."

"Jake? You want me to ask Jake about women? The lothario of Firehouse 173?"

Jake Doren, CJ's twin brother, popped his head around the hallway door, peering in at Danny and CJ. "Is someone maligning my reputation?"

CJ turned to stare at her brother. "Nope. I think Danny was sort of complimenting it."

Danny hit his forehead with his hand. "No offense, Jake, but I don't want tips on brushing a woman off, but getting her to stay."

Pursing his lips, Jake blew a long whistle. "*Whewwww,* that's a tough one, Dan. I've never had that problem."

Danny blew his hair off his forehead. "I can see you two won't be any help. I don't know why I asked you."

CJ and Jake started laughing. "Sorry."

"Did you want something, Jake?" Danny asked.

"Yeah, the chief wants you."

CJ punched her brother's arm. "I already told him."

Scowling at his sister, Jake rubbed his arm, then brightened. "Hey, why don't you ask the chief about it? Mike probably knows."

Danny just shook his head and walked to the door, leaving the twins arguing about who had that bright idea first. As far as he was concerned, asking Mike was a hopeless task. The guy was in his thirties and never married. He'd be as much help as Jake.

Chief Mike Crezinski's door was open, so he entered and closed it behind him.

"Sit down, Danny," Mike said, and then got straight to the

point. "You know that promotion we were talking about? It's off the table."

Danny winced. "Can I ask why?"

"I've decided that it will be better suited to Ron Sullivan."

"Ron? Why?"

"He's had some health problems and has to hang up his hoses. He's a good man and still has a lot of good years before retirement, so a daytime schedule with more desk work and preinspection would be the right thing for him."

"I didn't see that coming. I didn't know Ron was having that many problems. I understand your decision, Mike. Ron will do a good job," Danny said, trying to put a positive face on the situation. He'd have to tell Tessa that his hours wouldn't be changing as he'd indicated.

Mike leaned back in his chair and studied Danny across the desk. "Look, Danny, I know you were hoping for something with more convenient hours for your family, but that position isn't the right career move for you. I don't think you'd like it for long."

"I filled in when the previous supervisor was on leave and I didn't mind it."

"That's because you were filling in. Full-time, you'd be bored as hell." When Danny didn't say anything, Mike continued, "Come on, admit it. Could you sit in the supervisor's chair when the alarm went off without aching to hop on the truck?"

A reluctant chuckle burst from Danny's lips. "You've got a point. And I've got to admit that I've been wondering about that, too."

Mike grinned back. "It's too soon to say anything official yet, but there's something else in the works for you. It's better for your career and your talents. Trust me, I'm taking care of you."

"I know you are, Mike, and thanks for that. I mean it. You've been a great boss and a great friend."

"I'm still great on both counts," Mike commented, drawing

a laugh from Danny. Then in his usual straight-to-the-point way he peppered Danny with questions. "Meanwhile, how's everything going at home? Getting much time to work on that boat you're restoring? It should be easier with Tessa, right? How's it going with her?"

"It's good, really good. I work on the boat when I can, and Tessa and I have settled into a routine. I like her kids. She likes mine. I can work. She can work. It's all cool."

Mike leaned back in his chair. "So why do you flinch when you say her name?"

"Whose name?" Danny tried to form an innocent look—one that failed miserably, from his chief's reaction. Folding his hands, Mike directed a piercing blue gaze across the desk. Danny sighed. "I'm… Look, there's this attraction between us, but it's awkward. Tessa is an independent woman. At least, she's determined to be. One thing she made clear is she doesn't want to go back to the type of life Laurie led."

"You've lost me, Danny. What type is that?"

"A homemaker. A capable woman who gives up a potential career to stay home and create a warm, loving home for her husband and children."

"Tessa thinks there is something wrong with that?"

"No, hell, no. She said she admires women who are fulfilled doing that." Danny held up his hand as Mike started to interrupt. "I know, I know… It doesn't make sense to me, either. All I know is she says she was a corporate wife and she did all that perfect home stuff, was at her husband's beck and call, and she—I think her husband played— Oh hell, Mike. How should I know? Once women start talking about this emotional stuff, I don't know what to do." Unable to sit any longer, Danny leaped to his feet and paced the room. "Give me a fire any day. Fires you can figure out. You assess the situation, have a plan of attack and then you adapt to the circumstances, but women…" A frustrated Danny shoved both hands through his hair. "Hell if I know about women."

Mike burst out laughing. "Join the club, pal, join the club. When someone finds the key to women, I hope they sell copies. Now, get back to work. You'll figure it out."

DANNY WASN'T THE ONLY ONE brooding over that eventful kiss in the woods. Tessa was still unsettled. As always when she was upset, she visited Rhonda. There was nothing better than sharing a problem with your best friend for compassion, followed by a dose of Rhonda's usual bracing perspective.

"Let me get this straight," Rhonda said. "You and Danny engaged in a heavy make-out session on a blanket in the woods with the kids around?"

"What?" Tessa turned so abruptly from watering Rhonda's plants that she sloshed water onto the floor from the watering can. "We did not make out."

"What do you call it? Because from where I sit what you described was pretty hot and heavy."

"You make it sound so, so— Our clothes were still on."

With a reminiscent expression on her face, Rhonda settled back in her chair. "The best making out involves leaving the clothes on and using your imagination about what is underneath."

Tessa groaned. "You have sex on the brain."

"Well," Rhonda said in a reasonable tone, "that's the only place I'm getting any."

"What happened to that guy you were dating?"

Rolling her eyes, Rhonda replied, "No real chemistry. Why bother if there is no *umph* when you kiss him?"

"Umph?"

Rhonda frowned. "Tingle, thrill, that 'oh my God, I can't believe it,' feeling. Don't tell me you never had that."

Tessa turned back to Rhonda's pathetic plants and tried to change the subject. 'You have a black thumb, Rhonda. These plants must cringe every time you come near them."

Rhonda wasn't having any. "Don't try to distract me. You've never had that tingle with a man?"

Adopting an attitude with her hand on her hip, Tessa slowly turned to face her friend. "Don't be silly."

Rhonda leaned forward and stabbed an accusing finger at Tessa. "You're not answering my question. You sound like a politician."

"Well, in the beginning, Colin—"

Waving her answer aside, Rhonda said, "I don't care about Colin. Did you feel that tingle with Danny?"

Tessa sighed, knowing that if she didn't answer, Rhonda would keep hammering on her until she did. "You'd have to be dead and buried last year not to feel that with Danny."

Satisfied, Rhonda settled back in her chair again and motioned Tessa to a chair. "Leave those damn plants alone and sit down."

Knowing when she was beaten, Tessa placed the watering can on the floor and sat. She braced herself for Rhonda's curiosity. "Okay, I'm sitting."

"You told me what happened, but you didn't tell me how you felt."

Clasping her hands in her lap, Tessa imagined her lips meeting Danny's again, shivering at the memory. "It was...magical...and dangerous. Too dangerous. I didn't want to stop. I'm not sure what might have happened if the kids hadn't interrupted us."

Rhonda whistled. "Wow, that good, huh?"

Tessa sighed. "Better. That's why I have to do something about it."

Rhonda bounced so much she almost fell off her chair.

"Hot damn, now you're talking. What do you want to do? Do you want my help?"

"Yes, I do. I want you to fix me up with that guy you keep talking about."

Rhonda's jaw dropped. "You want me to what?"

"Arrange a date for me."

"What the hell for? You've got a sexy fireman panting to put out your fire and you want to date someone else?"

"Yes, it's the only way I can erect a wall between Danny and me. I'm going to tell him that I've been dating this guy for a while and…" Tessa hesitated for a moment. "And this way, Danny and I can go back to our business arrangement with no problems or upsets."

"Tessa, I think you have finally gone downriver, around the bend and over the falls. This is one of the most idiotic plans I've ever heard from you, and I've known you since the eighth grade. It's because of me…"

Tessa stood and began pacing. "Don't start. I know the story. I only moved here because you were here and I needed some support after Colin and I divorced. I appreciate everything you've done, so please do this for me, too." Tessa must have sounded more desperate than she thought, because Rhonda instantly got up and walked over to throw her arms around her.

"Okay, you can count on me. We'll try for next Saturday, so see if Danny is off to watch the kids."

"Danny? You mean you can't watch them? I mean, I talked to Danny about dating in the beginning, but things have changed now and I really think you would be—"

"Look, Tessa, regardless of the change in circumstances, it will be much better if Danny does," Rhonda replied with a sly look that Tessa instantly mistrusted.

"What are you up to?"

"Nothing."

"I don't believe you."

"I might have a hot date myself, so I want to leave the night open, that's all. What did you think I was up to?" Rhonda asked with her most innocent expression.

"I don't know. I just…" Tessa thrust her hands through her hair. "Okay, never mind. I have to go. I have an appointment after lunch. Let me know if—"

"Don't worry," Rhonda soothed. "I'll call you this afternoon."

TRUE TO HER WORD, an enthusiastic Rhonda called to inform Tessa that her date was set for Saturday. The news made Tessa more nervous than ever as she approached Danny's house to pick up her children that evening. As usual, Danny was sitting on the porch, but he had a beer in his hand instead of his usual lemonade. With a self-conscious wave she called, "Hi, Danny. How did it go today?"

He leaned back against the swing. "Let's see. Kids laughed, kids cried, General got out of the yard and dug up the neighbor's marigolds, Emma skinned her knee, Alison and I had a blowup and then she sulked around the house like a displaced princess. The boys climbed trees and started building a tree house, Kyle fell out of the tree just missing the box with the baby squirrel, who ran back up the tree and wouldn't come down, so Eric and Kevin climbed up after him only to have the squirrel leap to another tree, and finally, Josie talked us all to death. Same old, same old."

Tessa shifted from side to side, looked down at the floor, then around the porch as if she'd never seen it before. "Great, that's great."

Danny sent her a curious look. "It is? Did you hear what I said?"

Tessa looked around again. "What? Oh sure, sure I did."

Putting his drink down, Danny walked over and placed his hands on her shoulders. "Okay, look at me. What's wrong?"

Tessa met his eyes, but couldn't hold his gaze. "Uh, I'd like to go out Saturday night."

Danny just stared at her. "You would? Well, that's a surprise. After what happened, you've been—"

Tessa rushed into speech, tripping over her words. "Could you possibly babysit for me on Saturday night?"

"Huh?" Danny said, removing his hands from her shoulders.

"I checked your schedule and you're not on duty, right?"

Danny frowned, "Uh, right. I'm off Friday and Saturday. Why?"

"I've sort of got a date."

Openmouthed, he stepped back and stared at her. Finally he recovered enough to say, "You what?"

"I sort of…" Tessa crossed her fingers behind her back to protect herself from her lie. "There's this guy that I've been sort of seeing off and on for a while. He has this project he wants to talk to me about, and suggested we have dinner on Saturday. I can bring the kids over here, if that works better for you."

Danny rubbed his forehead. "How do you sort of see someone?"

"Uh, we go out every few months or so, like clockwork."

"Every few months?" Danny blinked. "Sounds rather premeditated, like flushing your plumbing system."

Tessa stiffened. "There's no need for insults." Tessa tried to avoid looking at him, because she knew Danny would see right through her lies if she continued. She could feel him staring at her. Sometimes Danny was too observant, but other times totally clueless, so maybe it would be all right.

"You're right." Danny backed off the conversation, trying to recover the comfortable feeling of a few minutes ago. He already had one woman, his teenage daughter, mad at him today. "Sorry, Tessa. It's been a long day. Forget I said anything." He walked back to the swing, with Tessa following right behind him. He bent to pick up his beer and took a long drink before placing it down and turning to say, "Sure I can babysit for you. Drop the kids off whenever. There's more room here than your condo. You can even have this guy meet you here if that's more convenient."

As her kids' voices drifted out to the porch, Tessa moved quickly toward the door, saying over her shoulder as Josie and Eric stepped through the doorway, "Thanks, I'll think about that. Josie, hold Fuzzface so he doesn't run into the street. Put him right into his cat carrier when we get in the car."

Danny rubbed his hands together. *Wait till this guy comes over. I'll make mincemeat of him.* He watched Tessa shoo her kids down the steps before he called, "Maybe you could return the favor?"

Tessa jerked to a stop. She whirled around to snap a look back at him. "Beg pardon?"

"You can watch my kids while I go out."

"I didn't know you were dating. Rhonda indicated—" She flushed. "That is…"

"Trust me," Danny said. "I'm not a monk. I've had my eye on the hottest little ole babe you've ever seen." He grinned to himself as Tessa slowly turned away from him and continued walking toward her car. He leaned on the railing. "I'll let you know when, okay?"

As Tessa waved in acknowledgment he wiped his brow. "Damn," he muttered, "where in the hell am I going to find a date?"

SATURDAY NIGHT TESSA TOOK great care to look her cool, sophisticated best for her date with Ted Willis. Inside was another story, however, as her stomach was churning faster than floodwaters. She tried to tell herself it was because of her date, but she knew it was actually because of Danny. She wanted him to look at her and hunger, which made no sense. She was the one who said their relationship should stay strictly business. Why should she wonder if she'd made the right decision now? *It doesn't work when you mix business with pleasure,* she thought, ignoring the tiny voice inside that reminded her that her ex-husband had always done exactly that and it didn't seem to hurt his job performance.

"Mommy, you're driving past Danny's house."

Josie's words recalled her attention to her driving. "Oops, sorry, I was thinking about something else."

"Like what, Mommy?"

"Quit asking questions, Josie," a sulky Eric ordered. "She has a *date.*"

The emphasis in Eric's voice didn't escape Tessa's attention. "Eric, we talked about this, didn't we? And what did you say?"

Eric scowled, but being a fair kid with maturity beyond his age, he said, "That I knew you were happier than you were before and so are me and Josie, so it's okay if you make a new life."

"That's right, that's what you said. Your father and I have been divorced for over a year. It's time for me to move on, and that includes seeing other people sometimes."

"You see people," Josie interjected. "You see Danny all the time. I like Danny, don't you like Danny, Mommy?"

Tessa parked the car while she answered, "Of course I like Danny. It's just that Danny and I—" Tessa stopped, not sure what else to say. She couldn't tell her young daughter exactly how much she liked Danny, nor did she want her son asking any more questions than he already had. She turned to finish answering Josie's question, but the twins and Emma racing toward the car had already diverted the child's attention. After one penetrating look at Tessa, her son decided to smile and get out of the car. Tessa watched as the swarm enveloped her children and swept them toward the house. There was no sign of Danny.

"Bye, have fun," she called, suddenly wishing she could join them. *That's no way to think,* she chided herself, and put the car in gear to meet Ted. She hadn't wanted to take the risk of asking Ted to pick her up at Danny's.

THREE HOURS LATER, Tessa was once again pulling up to the curb in front of Danny's house, but this time Ted was following her in his car. Tessa got out and walked over to her date. "You didn't have to follow me."

"Nonsense," Ted replied, sliding out of his own car and walking around to join her on the sidewalk. "I wanted to be sure you got home safely."

"That's so sweet. Thank you, Ted. I had a lovely time." With a smile she turned and began walking toward Danny's house, but stopped as a tug on her arm stopped her and she found herself linked with Ted. She glanced up at him. He was a good-looking man with light brown hair, humorous hazel eyes and a slightly out-of-shape physique. He'd been easy to talk to and amusing. Tessa had had a good time. Beyond that Tessa had felt nothing for him, except a slight shame that she was using him in the hopes that her feelings toward Danny would change.

"I insist on walking you to your door like a gentleman," Ted teased.

"It's not my door. It's my babysitter's door."

"No matter," Ted said, leading her up the walk toward the stairs. "I really had fun tonight, Tessa. I'm glad Rhonda arranged for us to meet."

"Shh," Tessa warned. It would be just like Danny to lurk by the door.

"What's the matter?" Ted whispered back. "Did I say something wrong?"

Tessa indicated the house. "No, they might be asleep."

Ted stared at the house that had been blazing with lights when they first pulled up. "It's only ten-thirty."

"I know. My babysitter is older and goes to bed early. I'm sorry we had to cut our date short tonight, but I really do need my beauty sleep. I've got to be at work early tomorrow."

Ted smiled. "Trust me, you don't need that beauty sleep at all." As he slipped his arms around her waist and leaned forward to kiss her, the porch light suddenly snapped on. The white glare was so intense that Tessa could have sworn Danny had switched the bulb to a higher wattage while she was gone. Before Tessa could say anything, the door swung open. Confronting them was a confident man exuding enough sex appeal in his well-fitting jeans and T-shirt to blast her date off the porch.

"Oh, Tessa, sorry, I didn't realize you were out here. I thought those raccoons were back again." If Danny's voice had gotten any more sugary she would have stuck to the porch.

Tessa untangled herself from Ted's arms, which wasn't hard, since he was staring at Danny as if he'd just glimpsed a jungle cat. At the gleam in Danny's eyes and the fierce smile, Tessa decided he wasn't too wrong. "Uh, Ted, this is Danny. Danny, Ted."

"How do you do," Ted replied, still with a stunned look on his face.

"I do fine, thanks," Danny said, with a suggestive look in Tessa's direction. "Every chance I get."

"Are you...I m-mean do you... Is he..." Ted stuttered as he looked from Tessa to Danny and back again.

Danny smiled. "I'm the babysitter. Tessa spends every spare minute here."

Outraged by his suggestion, Tessa tried to explain the situation to Ted, but he wasn't inclined to listen as he backed away, clearly uncomfortable.

"It's fine, Tessa. No problem. I didn't understand, sorry…. I think I'll take off and the two of you can do—" he shrugged as he moved toward the steps "—uh, do whatever you do. I'll call you, okay?" With as much dignity as he could muster, Ted galloped down the stairs and headed for his car.

A guilty Tessa called, "I really enjoyed tonight, Ted. I can't wait to see you again." Ted just waved and hopped into his car. Tessa turned and stalked toward the doorway. "Just what do you think you're doing?" she demanded of the man leaning against the doorjamb and trying hard to control a grin. "What gives you the right to ruin my date?"

"I didn't mean to ruin your date. I told you—I thought it was raccoons."

"Baloney!" Tessa exploded. "Don't try to get out of this with that charming smile. You knew there were no raccoons on your porch. Raccoons don't drive cars."

Danny rubbed his chin and stepped out onto the porch. "Well, you've got me there. Still, they're mighty smart little buggers."

"Stop it, just stop it. Where are my children? It's time to take them home."

"They just finished some pizza and are watching a movie. It's almost over."

"Then they'll have to finish it tomorrow. I need to get home." So she could lick her wounds in peace. The man had no right to look sexy as sin.

"How was your date?" Danny said, leaning back against the doorjamb. "Ted seemed like a nice guy."

"He was…is…I don't want to talk about my date."

"That bad, huh? Sorry about that. Sometimes the chemistry just doesn't work."

"Danny, I am not discussing chemistry with you."

"Good, 'cause I suck at chemistry."

Tessa narrowed her eyes at his statement. "You're not fooling me, you know. You're deliberately trying to unsettle me."

"Why would I want to do that?" Danny asked, tucking a stray wisp of hair behind Tessa's ear.

Tessa slapped his hand away. "So I will hop into bed with you."

Danny's eyes were twinkling even as he tried to look solemn. "Tessa, have you forgotten that our relationship is strictly business?"

"Association," she snapped. "Relationship sounds too… Anyway, I don't want to talk to you anymore. Please ask my children to come out here immediately." Danny just smiled and stared at her a few moments longer, as if he was memorizing her, as if he'd never seen her before. Tessa was torn between wanting to stiffen and a desire to throw herself into his arms. Why did he have to be so appealing? She folded her arms and tapped her toe. "Now, please."

"I love that little black number you're wearing, sweetheart."

Tessa's tense shoulders were practically up to her ears as she tried to avoid encouraging him to go further. "Danny…my kids. Now."

Danny only smiled, kissing his fingers before placing them on her lips. "Someone who looks so sexy should be kissed good-night."

Tessa could feel the burning his simple touch created and deliberately fished in her bag for her keys. "Send Eric and Josie out. I'll be in the car."

"Tessa." Danny's voice was hot fudge and twice as inviting. "I'll be over at five-fifteen tomorrow to watch the kids."

THE NEXT TWENTY-FOUR HOURS passed without incident for Tessa and the children. It wasn't until Danny came home the next morning that the nerves he'd started arousing with his touch kicked into full gear. A weary-looking Danny nodded at Tessa and went straight to the coffeepot.

"Long day?" Tessa asked, looking up from her coffee and the newspaper.

"We had two calls last night. I didn't get much rest."

"Nothing serious, I hope."

"Everything we get is serious," he snapped.

"I'm sorry," Tessa, said, taken aback by his tone, "I didn't mean to suggest…"

"Forget it. Sorry, I overreacted." He took a sip of coffee. "One was a traffic accident, minor injuries. The other was a fire that we caught before it did too much damage." Danny leaned back against the counter and sipped his coffee. With each sip he looked a bit more alert. "Oh, I forgot to tell you. The chief told me a few days ago that I didn't get that promotion, so there won't be a change in hours."

"Oh Danny, I'm sorry. You must be so disappointed."

"Not really. Mike made the right decision. I would have gotten bored. He said something else is coming up for me, something better." Danny yawned, opening his mouth wide. "Sorry, shouldn't you be taking off?"

Tessa drained her coffee and stood. "Yes, I guess so. I have to locate some plants today, so I'll be on the road a lot."

"How's business going?"

"They say the second year is always harder than the first." What she didn't reveal to him was the state of her finances, which were fast approaching the help-wanted stage. She wondered if she should start thinking of approaching Colin for more child support. She'd discovered just how expensive it could be for a single parent.

"If you need a loan—"

Unwilling to drop her worries on Danny's shoulders, she

said, "No, no, it's just tight at the moment. Don't worry. I'll come up with something." She smiled and waved as she headed to the front door. Danny's voice stopped her.

"Would you watch the kids Friday night?"

She turned to face Danny, who was standing in the kitchen doorway, eyes steady on hers as he sipped his coffee. "Friday? Sure, sure, no problem. Do you want me to come over here?"

"That would be good."

"Okay, you've got it. Friday it is."

Chapter Eight

When Tessa, Eric and Josie showed up on Friday night, they found Danny in a well-cut navy blue suit complemented by a light gray shirt and patterned tie. He looked as if he'd just wandered in from the pages of *GQ*. Tessa's breath came a bit faster as she looked him over. *I wonder who the lucky girl is.* She didn't ask, because she was suddenly unwilling to know.

"Why are you staring at me? Did I nick myself shaving? Leave my fly open?" He automatically checked to make sure the zipper was up.

"Huh?" Tessa jolted out of her daydream. "Oh, no. You look nice."

"Thank you. I do clean up every once in a while, you know."

"So I see."

After a searching glance at her, Danny checked his watch. "I have to go. I don't want to keep my date waiting."

"No, of course not. Where are your kids?"

"They're around somewhere. Rustle a bag of chips and they'll come."

"I'll do that." Tessa smiled, followed him to the door and gave him a little push. "Go on, get out of here. Have fun." Tessa had never had to work harder at sounding casual in her entire life, but she was pleased with the result when Danny waved and headed for his car.

Tessa had to stop herself from following him as she realized she'd have to spend the rest of the evening pretending to the kids that nothing was wrong. Truthfully, she wasn't sure what was wrong. She couldn't be jealous of Danny dating someone, not when she'd taken great pains to convince him that her interest was only as a child-care provider and that his kisses were unwelcome. But his kisses were more welcome than she wanted to admit. Her musing was interrupted as the twins came clattering down the stairs followed by an angry Alison close behind.

"I'm going to kill you guys if you don't stay out of my room."

The two boys dashed behind Tessa for protection. "No, you ain't."

"Aren't," Tessa automatically replied. "No, you aren't."

The boys stuck out their tongues at their sister and crowed, "See, she said you aren't."

"I didn't…I was correcting your grammar. Besides, the only one who is doing any killing around here is me." She turned to Alison. "Okay, what's this all about?"

"They came to my room and went into my underwear drawer and they—" Alison was so angry she was turning purple and couldn't finish her answer.

Turning to take a better look at the boys, Tessa noticed for the first time the underpants and bras they were wearing over their clothes. Despite their obvious guilt they managed to look innocent. Tessa had no idea how the twins did it, but it was effective. A small laugh escaped before she steeled her expression to disapproval.

"Tessa, don't laugh. You said I could come to you, but you lied. You're like all the other women who want to get close to my dad by being nice to me."

"Alison, I'm sorry. I didn't mean to laugh. And that isn't why I'm nice to you."

"You're always flirting with Dad and making him flirt back. I saw you at the picnic. I saw what happened when we weren't there." Alison almost spit the last sentence at Tessa.

Tessa was mortified by the accusation, but before she could respond, Kyle and Kevin interrupted the conversation.

"Look, we're hula dancers," they announced, wiggling around the room.

"You two take those clothes off immediately," Tessa ordered. Instead of obeying, the boys danced around the room, which inspired Alison to scream, "I hate all of you," and chase after them.

Into this commotion strolled Eric, obviously alerted by the chaos regardless of the headphones plugging his ears. "What's going on?"

"We've got Alison's underwear," the twins taunted. "She wears bikinis."

Alison stopped running, gave Eric one quick embarrassed look and burst into tears. "My life is ruined," she wailed.

Then Josie and Emma wandered down the stairs wearing princess costumes. "I thought you guys were going to play dress-up with us."

The twins giggled. "We are. We're pretending we're Alison."

Now it all made sense to Tessa. Shaking the last of her inertia away, she took control. "Boys, take Alison's things off right now or you will be sent to bed without supper."

The threat of no food worked. The twins stripped faster than a porn star and dropped the clothes on the floor. "Now pick them up and hand them to your sister with an apology and a promise never to do this again." The boys tried their innocent smile, but this time it didn't work. Tessa gave them the stone-face stare that mothers learn the minute they have children. Resigned, the boys picked up the clothes and handed them to Alison with a reluctant "Sorry."

"Repeat after me," Tessa said. "I will never take Alison's clothes again under pain of having no cookies for six months."

"Six months!" the twins yelled.

"Six months," Tessa replied in her sternest voice and stood with arms crossed as they repeated the promise. "Kyle, Kevin, go to your room and get ready for bed."

"Bed!" they wailed. "Already?"

"Go."

"Eric, Josie, Emma, go back to what you were doing." Tessa watched as the children trailed away, leaving her with Alison.

Tessa walked over to Alison and tried to take her hand, but Alison jerked it away. "I want to go to my room."

"Alison, I'm sorry. I don't know what I've done to make you think I'm using you, but…"

Alison gave Tessa a surprisingly adult look, but said nothing. Tessa tried again. "Alison, please, let's talk about this."

"There's nothing to talk about. I'd like to be excused to put my things away."

Since Alison wasn't going to speak to her about her accusation, Tessa tried a new topic. "Your brothers were just teasing you. Try not to take it so hard."

Alison glared at her. "I hate my brothers."

"I can see why. But they're just little boys."

"Quit taking their side. They're dumb and totally clueless."

Tessa couldn't help smiling. "I have news for you, honey— some of them don't change even when they grow up."

Alison sent her a stormy but interested look. "Really?"

"Really. Go ahead, take your things upstairs. If you feel like coming back later, we can make popcorn balls."

Alison merely shrugged her shoulders and climbed the stairs, heaving a dramatic sigh.

Tessa watched Alison leave, tempted to go after her, but knowing the best thing to do was leave her alone. Still, she was very disturbed by what the girl had said. How many women tried to get close to Danny through Alison, she wondered. Tessa bit her lip. And then there was the flirting accusation, which involved too much truth to deny. She could deny it to Alison, but she'd have a harder time denying it to herself. Not that she was the only one at fault; Danny had to take his share of the blame for the situation. Hard as they tried, they couldn't seem to kill the sparks between them. She was much better off trying to stay away from him. Under the circumstances, though, she had no hope of making that a reality. Maybe his date tonight would change the situation. But even as Tessa thought that, she prayed it wouldn't. Finally she gave up, as a pain began pounding in her temples. Tessa squeezed her eyes tight for a minute and then rushed to the kitchen to find a pain reliever. She had one hell of a headache!

Somehow they all made it through the evening, with Alison relenting and joining everyone downstairs. Tessa figured it wasn't fun to be a martyr when there was no one around to see. She had allowed the twins to come down in their pajamas, and Alison reluctantly forgave her brothers when they finally made a sincere apology after five attempts. But she was still cool to Tessa, which made Tessa's head start pounding again.

After the children had gone to their rooms for the night a few hours later, Tessa tried to settle down with a book. It was no good. She kept listening for the sound of a car pulling into the driveway. She threw the book down and restlessly wandered the house. She loved this place. It was a bit worn and as messy as her condo was neat and orderly, but that didn't bother her. This house felt happy and well loved. There was a warmth that lingered even when no one was there, inviting everyone to put their feet up and relax. It was completely different from the homes where she'd grown up and the homes she had shared with Colin. They'd been more like stage sets where she was just another display prop.

When she finally heard a car door slam she forced herself not to race to the door and peer outside. As footsteps sounded on the porch, Tessa flung herself into a chair and picked up her book. She didn't look up even when the door squeaked.

"Hi," Danny said.

Tessa gave an exaggerated jump that wouldn't have fooled a first grader. She peered over her book. "Oh, you startled me."

"Good book?" Danny asked as he casually strolled over to stand in front of her.

"It's great. I can't stop reading it."

"Do you always read books upside down?"

"What?" Tessa glanced down. She turned the book right side up. "Okay, you caught me. I wanted to see if you'd notice."

"Why?"

Why is right. "No reason. Just a silly impulse." Tessa tried to play off the comment with a carefree chuckle.

Danny rubbed the side of his nose as he studied her. "You don't do things on impulse. You plan every minute."

"I do not."

"Sure you do. If you ask me, you could use more impulse in your life."

That comment stung. Tessa snapped her book closed and leaned forward. "Unlike you, I'm focused."

Danny laughed. "I'm focused. I just like to relax and be loose every once in a while." To emphasize his point he unbuttoned his collar button and loosened his tie.

"I relax. Who says I don't relax?"

"Are you relaxed now?"

Tessa clenched her fists, feeling the blood pounding in her temples. First Alison had blindsided her with accusations and now Danny was tormenting her. She wanted to take a swing at the self-confident jerk. Her voice rose, "What's the matter with you? The kids are in bed and I'm sitting here reading a book. Of course I'm relaxed. I'm damn relaxed."

"Hmm." Danny stepped forward with a smile and lifted her out of the chair to stand on her feet. He retained his light grip on her arms. "How about now?" He pulled her closer. "Or now?"

Tessa stumbled forward, stopping herself before she was enveloped in his arms. "How was your date with the hot babe?"

Danny let her go so fast she almost fell back on the chair. "Date. Right. Great, it was great. Connie was great."

There was silence for a moment, leaving Tessa perplexed by the sudden tension. "I'd better get my kids home."

"Why don't you leave them here? You'll be back tomorrow anyway when I'm back on duty."

"Well, I suppose that would be all right."

"You're welcome to spend the night, too."

The sexual danger inherent in that remark sharpened Tessa's response. "I don't want to impose."

At that, Danny made a noise that sounded like a chuckle and a groan at the same time. "I wish you would impose."

Tessa's breath caught at the almost hungry expression in his eyes. She fumbled for something to say. "I'm sure the Great Connie wouldn't agree to my spending the night alone in the house with you."

Danny yanked at his tie. "Connie is..."

Tessa waited, but he didn't go on. "Is?" she prompted.

"Is, uh, is..." Danny stumbled over his words and looked at the ceiling.

"Connie is what?" Tessa asked again, praying he wouldn't begin cataloguing her virtues.

"Is understanding...about other women—my seeing other women, I mean."

Tessa snorted. "Trust me, no woman is that understanding."

"No, no, it's all right, really it is. I could ask you out, for instance, and she wouldn't bat an eye."

With a skeptical laugh, Tessa challenged, "Prove it. Call and ask her. I'm betting she has your gizzards for breakfast."

"Do people have gizzards? I thought only chickens had gizzards."

Taken completely off guard by his sudden switch of topics, Tessa could only gape at him.

Danny grinned. "If I hadn't seen you at a complete loss for words, I wouldn't have believed it."

Tessa attempted to gather her dignity. "Well, I only hope Connie appreciates your sense of humor."

"Connie and I don't talk a lot when we go out," he said with a provocative look in his eyes.

Tessa tried to bury the sudden spurt of jealousy his words aroused. "That's…I'd rather not have more detail about your personal life, thank you very much."

He stepped a little bit closer and whispered, "Jealous?"

Tessa stepped around him. "Absolutely not. I have no reason to be jealous. Our arrangement is strictly professional."

Danny folded his arms as he looked her over. "Still time to change it. Tempted?"

Tessa had finally had enough. "I'll be back tomorrow morning." She stalked across the room and picked up her purse before turning at the door to face him. "You know, I find it very hard to believe that you have the nerve to go out on a date and then come home and proposition me. What type of behavior is that?"

"Tessa, I was just joking. I wasn't serio—"

"Then why do it?"

Danny shrugged, looking helpless as he searched for an answer. "I don't know. It's so tempting to tease you and force you off balance when you're so serious and determined most of the time."

"You know what, Danny Santori? Alison was right. You are a Neanderthal."

A FEW DAYS LATER Rhonda leaned across the counter in the momentarily quiet E.R. at Warenton General Hospital and asked Tessa, "So what did Danny say when you called him a Neanderthal?"

Tessa hit the counter with the palm of her hand. "He didn't say anything. He just looked smug and then he laughed. He's probably back there now cleaning his animal skin and oiling his club."

"You've got to remember, hon, he's a fireman. They're kind of—how can I put this?" Rhonda tapped her front tooth with her fingernail. "They're a testosterone-heavy breed of man. That's why they get the job done, and why we love them."

"I didn't say I loved Danny." Tessa bristled.

"I was speaking generally."

"Oh, sorry," Tessa muttered.

Rhonda came around the desk and leaned her elbow on the high counter. "But you were pretty quick with the denial there, old friend. So what is going on between you? I've never known you to get this riled up except when you found out about Colin's affairs, but that was understandable."

"Oh, Rhonda, I don't know what's going on. He flirts with me and I don't mean to, but I respond."

"Who can blame you? Danny's delicious to look at, funny, charming, financially solvent and most of all unattached."

Tessa fisted her knuckles on her hips and glared at the smaller woman. "Rhonda, do you think I walked away from Colin to be independent just so I could fall into a relationship with another man, especially one who's like...like...like..."

"Danny?"

"Yes." Tessa stared at her friend for a long moment. "Ah hell, Rhonda, what am I going to do?"

"I don't know, but if it wasn't for all those kids, I would have tackled Danny Santori a long time ago."

"Oh, that's another problem. Yesterday I had a very unpleasant encounter with Alison." She proceeded to tell her about the incident, waiting until Rhonda stopped laughing at the boys in Alison's underwear so she could continue. "She saw me kissing her father at the picnic, and now she hates me, doesn't trust me, thinks I'm after her father…."

"Well, aren't you?"

"No. Not the way she means it. Oh, Rhonda, I'm so confused."

"Your response I don't know about, but Alison's response seems natural for a child who has lost her mother. She's trying to hang on to her daddy so he won't leave her, too."

"I know. I understand that and I'm trying to be sympathetic, but she's making it very hard. She's so difficult."

"Well, she—" Rhonda began, then she broke off and started waving at someone down the hall. "Here comes someone who knows more than we do."

Tessa turned to look at the petite curly-haired woman practically dancing in their direction. "Tessa, this is Beth Simmons. She's a master's candidate in child psychology and is working here part-time. She's Chief Mike Crezinski's sister. Beth, this is Tessa Doherty."

"Hi, Tessa," Beth said with a huge grin.

Rhonda stared at her. "Beth, did you get into the medicine closet or something? You're awfully happy."

Beth thrust her left hand forward. "I'm engaged. He popped the question a few minutes ago."

With a smile, Tessa examined the diamond. "That's lovely.

I hope you'll be very happy." She started to move away from Beth and Rhonda. "I'll let you two get back to work."

Rhonda grabbed her arm. "Not so fast. I want you to tell Beth about Alison. Tessa watches Danny Santori's kids when he's working and he watches hers when she's at work."

"Mmm-hmm." Beth nodded. "So what's up with Danny Delicious?"

For the second time Tessa repeated the story as an attentive Beth listened. "I was hoping Rhonda might have some suggestions," Tessa finished.

"Have you told Danny about this?" Beth asked.

"No. I didn't think it a good idea. It might just make him mad at her and that's the last thing she needs from her dad. I'd like to handle this myself."

"Good plan. Well, from what I've heard from firehouse gossip, a number of women have tried to use Ali to meet her father. There was a Marilyn someone who taught Alison gymnastics, I think. I don't know what happened, but Ali quit gymnastics and Marilyn turned her baby blues on my brother, Mike."

"What do you think Tessa should do, Beth?" Rhonda asked.

"Why don't you try getting Alison involved in something you like that she might like, also? What do you do?"

"I'm a landscape designer." Tessa thought for a moment. "I know Alison is into fashion, like most young teenagers, so maybe I can find a way to use that."

"There you go. Let her spend time with you so she feels important and starts trusting that you like her for herself."

Rhonda agreed. "That's a good idea, Beth. Then your only problem will be Danny, Tessa."

"Why?" Beth looked from one to the other. "How is Danny a problem?"

As Tessa opened her mouth to answer, the sound of a siren getting closer captured everyone's attention. The phone behind the desk rang and Rhonda leaned over to answer it, listening a minute before replacing the receiver. She turned to the E.R. staff and bellowed, "Rest time is over. Incoming. A three-car pileup on the interstate."

What had been a quiet space a moment ago now resembled a frantic beehive. Tessa stepped back and bumped against Beth, who was moving behind her on her way down the hall.

"See you later, Tessa. Good luck." With a brisk wave Beth raced up the hallway.

"Bye, Rhonda," Tessa called.

Rhonda looked up from preparing a suture tray. "Hey, I forgot to ask, did you ever reach Colin after he called you the other night?"

"No, we're playing telephone tag. I'll try him again tonight." With a wave she left the hospital wondering what on earth her ex-husband could want, since he was supposed to be in the Bahamas on vacation. When she tried to call him back that evening there was no answer, so Tessa decided not to dwell on it. If Colin really needed to get in touch he'd find a way, since no one was more single-minded in achieving his own objectives than her ex-husband. It's what had made him so successful in business. And so terrible in their marriage.

Chapter Nine

Sitting at Danny's table one afternoon near the end of October, Tessa stared at her bank balance. If she didn't get some new contracts soon, she might have to look for a job and continue developing her business on the side. Either that or dip into the account that Colin's lawyer had finally set up in her name. Tessa considered that account blood money and had vowed not to touch it unless it was necessary for the children. She realized her attitude wasn't logical, as she had definitely earned a stipend after thirteen years of marriage, but that's how she felt.

With a huge sigh she snapped the checkbook closed and reached for a flyer her new friend Barrett had given her that week. The flyer advertised a holiday event from the same people who promoted the spring home and garden show. Barrett had recommended she enter the event and consider it money well spent. He was probably right, Tessa decided, reaching for the application form. Once that chore was completed she pulled her sketchbook toward her and started designing. An hour later she stared at her idea and noticed Alison hovering by the kitchen door.

"Hi, Alison."

Alison crunched on her apple as she studied Tessa. "What are you doing?"

"Designing a holiday display."

Alison sipped her water. "For a client?"

"I wish," Tessa answered. "Clients have been rather thin on the vine, so I've decided to enter Scents of the Season to find some."

"When's that?"

"Right after Thanksgiving. It's going to be tons of work and I'm not sure if I can pull it off."

Alison moved closer, pointing at the paper. "Can I see that?"

When Tessa hesitated, Alison hunched her shoulders and extended a sulky lip. "Never mind, forget it."

Tessa stood up. "Wait, don't go. I hesitated because I think it sucks. Take a look and tell me what you think." Tessa pulled out the chair next to her, then sat and slid the sketch over to Alison.

Alison studied it for a few minutes. "Is this supposed to be a sleigh ride or something?"

Tessa nodded. "Pretty lame, huh? I blanked out on an idea."

Alison took a sip of water. "Why don't you do something magical?"

"Like what?"

With a shy expression Alison ducked her head, staring at the sketch. "Did you read that really old book about the secret garden when you were a kid?"

"Back in the old days before the Internet was created, you mean?" Tessa teased.

Alison flushed. "Uh, yeah, I guess so. I read my mom's copy from when she was little. Mom loved books."

"Did she? I do, too," Tessa confessed. "How about you?"

Alison's tone was defensive. "Yeah, but don't tell anybody. I don't want to come off like a geek or something."

"It's our secret." Tessa nodded. "But Alison, loving to read isn't geeky. It takes you into new worlds you never knew existed."

"It's geeky when everyone else is into video games and stuff like that."

Since there was nothing Tessa could say to that, she went back to the original subject. "What about the book?"

"You could do a secret garden, a holiday garden for fairies. We could have little places for fairies to hide among the plants and decorations. We could make these little fairy figures and dress them up."

Tessa tapped her pencil on her sketch pad. "Hmm."

"Never mind. It was dumb idea."

Tessa was thoughtful, remembering Beth Simmons's suggestion of involving Alison in a project. "No, I like it."

"You do?"

Tessa flipped to a blank page and started sketching. "I really do. Let's see now… We could do an L-shaped stone wall as the backdrop and add some old-fashioned garden flowers, shrubs and trees. We can do it as a winter garden."

"Oh, wait," Alison continued, really getting into it. "We can do more than winter. What about adding fall and summer and—the fairies could dress—"

"For each season?" Tessa interrupted, beginning to see the possibilities.

Alison was almost bouncing in her seat. "Wouldn't that be awesome?"

"Hmm," Tessa said, tapping her pencil against her lips. "Let's see, we can still get the autumn flowers easily, spring probably at a greenhouse, but summer might be a challenge."

"We can paint the branches and add fake leaves and flowers or something, couldn't we?" Alison was really getting into the idea. "And we can do snow and glitter for winter, stuff like that."

"Alison, this sounds great, but it would be a ton of work in a very short time. We'd only have four or five weeks, because the show runs in six weeks and I'd have to set up in advance and have our exhibit approved and...I don't know if I can pull it off."

"I could help, if you want. And maybe Eric would, 'cause he's older. Maybe I can find some other people. Or you could just do your own thing. It doesn't matter to me," Alison added, covering her previous enthusiasm with a bored look. "I don't really care."

"Oh, no," Tessa said in a light tone as she recognized Alison's turnabout as a way to disguise her insecurity. "You came up with this great idea, so now you're stuck, kid."

Alison shrugged. "I guess I could."

Tessa reached into her tote bag, pulled out some gardening books she'd bought the day before and placed them on the table. "Are you sure you'll have time to work with me, since you're back in school?"

"I guess so."

Tessa hid a smile at Alison's attempt at nonchalance. "If it's going to take away from anything you might be doing after school or on the weekends, like sports or clubs, then you can stop."

Alison shrugged. "I'm not doing much of that yet, just soccer."

After a moment Tessa asked, "How's high school?"

"Okay."

"A lot of your friends from middle school are there, too, right?"

"Some. Some I wish weren't."

Tessa stopped sketching and glanced at Alison. "Why?"

Alison buried her face in one of Tessa's gardening books, staring as intently as if she'd never seen a plant before.

"Alison?"

"Look, this flower is pretty."

Tessa glanced over. "Those are coral bells—see the shape? They grow during summer into fall."

"So we could use them for our garden?"

"We can. Good choice, Alison. They're happy flowers." Tessa waited a moment, and then asked, "Are you having a problem with anyone?"

Alison hesitated, continuing to look at the book. Finally she said, "Marti has been my best friend since the third grade, but now she's hanging around with some new girls she met at the beginning of the year."

"Did you meet them, too?"

"Yeah. They know a lot of people at the high school, not just freshmen. They get a lot of attention from everyone. And somehow Marti made friends with them."

"Ahhh." Tessa nodded. "The queen bees, if that's what you call them now. I never fit in with them."

Alison turned to her with a stunned look. "You didn't? But you're so…I mean, you look like a model—tall, slender, really pretty with beautiful clothes."

Tessa laughed as she looked down at her khaki shorts and light blue denim shirt. "Yes, I look ready for the runway at the moment."

Alison smiled. "It doesn't matter what you're wearing. Somehow you just always give that impression."

"Well, thanks for the compliment."

Alison shrugged. "I hope I'll look as good as you one day."

"Oh, honey, you already do." It was so heartbreaking to see this young girl on the verge of womanhood, knowing she had so many wonderful and painful times to experience on the way. Tessa wanted to hold Alison tight and soothe away her fears, but she sensed that would be unwelcome.

"Alison, the thing about high school is you have to try to fit in without losing yourself. You have to be true to your personality, values and interests. That can be very hard. It's always tempting to pretend you're someone else."

"You think Marti has the right idea?"

Tessa risked smoothing Alison's hair back from her face. "No, I don't, but I understand why she's doing it."

"But she's been practically ignoring me for those other girls."

"I wouldn't worry about Marti, Alison. It's easy to be dazzled when you're not sure who you are yet. If she's a real friend she'll be back."

Alison didn't look totally convinced, but Tessa felt she'd given her something to think about. She steered the conversation back to their design. "What about a secret entrance to get into the garden? Any ideas?"

"A tunnel?"

Tessa laughed. "I can just see all the little old ladies crawling through it at the show."

Alison giggled. "Maybe it wouldn't be such a good idea. Oh, I know—how about an old wooden door that's propped open?"

"We could have old-fashioned roses or bushes on each side," Tessa agreed, starting to sketch again. "We could actually only do one larger display, but as you walk through the garden it changes from fall to winter to spring to summer every few feet. That way we can build the garden structure one time and make the plants change as we walk the path."

"It has to be a brick path, like those old paths you see in movies."

With key elements decided, Alison and Tessa started checking the garden books and designing the garden layout. They decided that Tessa would pick Alison up the next day and they would look for plant sources while Danny stayed with the other kids. Tessa couldn't wait to tell Danny all about it, which surprised her. There was no way she could see him appreciating a fairy garden with the enthusiasm she and Alison were showing.

As usual, he surprised her with his support for the idea the next day when she arrived to pick up Alison.

"You're going to enter that new holiday show? Good for you. What are you going to do? I couldn't understand Alison's note." He pulled it out of his pocket, peering at it. "It's something about elves or trolls...."

"Fairies, it's about fairies. It's a Secret Fairy Garden. Alison is going to help me with the display. She's trying to find some other people, too, since we don't have a lot of time."

"Alison's going to help?" Danny raised an eyebrow. "I know what a brat she's been to you. What did you do, give her a magic potion?"

"I know. I was as surprised as you are when she got excited about it. The secret garden was her idea."

"Let's hope her interest holds," Danny said with a doubtful look. "So who else can help you? Rhonda?"

"Rhonda is already on board, and so is this woman I met at the hospital, Beth Simmons. Rhonda said you know her?"

"She's my fire chief's sister—adopted sister, really."

Tessa nodded and told Danny more about her plans and the short time frame she had to complete the project.

"I can ask around the firehouse and see if anyone knows people good at doing crafts. I can also call Connie. She's good with her hands and loves to—" He stopped suddenly.

With a skeptical arch in her voice, Tessa said, "Connie?"

Danny practically scuffed his feet as he avoided Tessa's gaze. "Maybe that wouldn't be such a great idea."

Tessa's expression grew even haughtier as she agreed. "Maybe not."

Danny quickly changed the subject. "Hey, you don't have room at your condo, so you can make this house your staging area. We can put everything under the deck in the back until we're ready to assemble the display."

"Thank you. That's a good idea and would help a lot."

Tessa was surprised by his enthusiasm, especially after Alison came down the steps and joined in the conversation. Soon Eric and Josie, followed by the other kids, wandered in, and before Tessa knew it, she had a team assembled at no cost to her—not that she expected any help from the little ones, but it did add to the excitement. By the time they finished their impromptu meeting it was as if she'd been run over by a freight train. She was amazed at how fast things were coming together. Now she just had to find the plants and materials to do the job.

ONLY TWO WEEKS REMAINED before the show. Tessa was erecting a trial display outside under a canvas tarp Danny had put up to protect her work while it was in progress. She had just picked up a fieldstone to move over to her wall when Danny strolled under the canvas.

"Hello."

Tessa jumped and bobbled the fieldstone. When she lost her battle to hold the stone, Danny grabbed her waist and yanked her backward. The rock dropped, just missing her foot.

"You okay?"

"Danny, you have to stop sneaking up on me."

Danny grinned. "What do you want me to do—wear tap shoes?"

Tessa chuckled at the thought. "I'd pay to see that."

"Keep saving, babe."

Tessa knelt to pick up the rock, but Danny elbowed her aside. "Here, I'll get it. Tell me where you want it."

Indicating the layer of stones she'd laid earlier, Tessa watched as Danny placed the stone in position. "Thank you."

"How much longer are you going to work today?"

"I don't know. My ex, Colin, showed up with no warning to see the kids this morning. He took them overnight and is bringing them back Sunday morning, so I plan to put that time to good use."

"You've been working pretty hard as it is. Why don't you knock off for the rest of the afternoon? I have something I'd like to show you." Without waiting for her answer, Danny took her hand and led her around the house.

"Danny. I have a schedule and I haven't finished what I—"

"Tessa, I understand schedules. I live on one, too. But every once in a while you need to let it all go and cut class."

"I've never cut class."

Danny laughed and steered her toward his car. "I'm not surprised."

"Wait, my bag."

"Where is it? I'll get it."

"Right inside the front door."

"I'll be right back." He jogged toward the house, emerging a minute later with her tote bag. He tossed it in the window at her before bounding around to the other side to slide behind the steering wheel and start the car.

"Wait, we can't go."

"Sure we can," Danny said, putting the car into gear and pulling into the street.

"You can't just go away and leave all your children alone."

"They aren't here."

"What? Where are they?"

"Alison is shopping with a friend and spending the night at her house. Kyle, Kevin and Emma went to a game and are going to dinner with some old friends and their kids. No one will be home until later this evening. We'll be back by then."

"I certainly hope so. I have things—"

"To do, I know. Just sit back and enjoy the ride."

After a bewildered look at Danny, Tessa leaned back and began to savor the scenery and the breeze from the open windows flowing through her hair. Fall was her favorite season. The trees were still carrying some color on this sunny day, but underneath the warmth was a hint of crispness warning of cooler days.

With an impatient wiggle, Tessa said, "Okay, give, where are we going?"

"We're almost there," Danny said, turning onto a side road that led toward Chicamongee Lake. He maneuvered the winding road and pulled into a parking spot by a boat dock. He turned off the key and stretched his arm along the back of the seat. "Ready for an adventure?"

Tessa stepped onto the gravel lot and waited for Danny to join her; surprised to see he was now carrying a large wicker basket. "What are you up to, Danny Santori?"

"You are the lucky one who is going to help me christen my new baby." Danny waved his hand toward a sailboat and gave Tessa a little push to get her moving. "This beauty is *Santori's Gang.* I bought it two years ago, but only started restoring her last year."

"This is the project you've been working on in your spare time?"

"This is it. Today is the first time I'm taking her out."

The closer Tessa got to the boat the more impressed she was. The sailboat was large enough to have a cabin for overnight trips but not so large as to be overwhelming. Danny led her proudly down the dock to the stairs onto the vessel.

"You should have seen it when I first bought it. I almost cried when I saw the condition of the deck and the rails. They're teak and it was a crime to let this beautiful wood go to ruin the way the old owner did."

"You did all of this yourself?" Tessa asked, looking around.

"Yep. First I had to fix the hull and then scrape so I could paint. Then I redid the inside…the sleeping bunks, galley and the head. I refinished the deck and all of the decorative wood last. It took months to get the finish I wanted, but I got it done a few weeks ago and put it in the water, even though it's so late in the season."

"So why haven't you taken the boat out?"

"I was waiting."

Tessa could feel herself blushing. "For what?"

"The right person who would appreciate it."

"You should take your children. They'd be thrilled to go."

"They'll go a lot, but there's only one first time."

"Like sex." Tessa froze. She couldn't believe that had come out of her mouth.

Laughing, Danny placed the basket on one of the benches. "I remember the girl, but it was over so fast I don't quite remember much else."

"I thought it was going to be better, too," Tessa confessed, wrinkling her nose.

Danny studied her for a moment. "Now, that's a subject I wouldn't mind exploring after we get under way."

"Forget it. That subject is closed."

Danny sent her a smile that tingled her toes. "We'll see."

Tessa couldn't leave it at that. "I mean it. Closed subject."

Without another word, Danny turned and started working with the sails. "Have you ever been sailing?"

"Unlike canoeing, I've sailed a number of times. My father had a small yacht. Of course, it was generally used for entertaining his clients while we were docked, but we did take it out sometimes, too."

"Then I'm going to put you to work. How about being the first mate?"

"Well, it's your boat. You're the captain, so first mate is acceptable, sir."

"I'm going to remember this moment," Danny said with a grin, "I don't think I've ever heard you so subservient before."

"You didn't hear it now. You heard me following the rules of the sea."

"If that's the way you need to think about it, fine by me. I'll hoist anchor and you grab that line." He pointed to the coiled ropes, then stopped her as she moved toward one. "No, not that one. You want the halyard to raise the mainsail."

Tessa snapped her fingers and moved to one of the other coiled lines. "How easily you forget when you're away from it for too long."

Danny winked. "Don't worry, they say that having sex again is like riding a bike." He laughed at Tessa's expression. "If that's any consolation."

"Who said anything about having sex?"

"You did, a few minutes ago."

"I didn't say I wanted to…to…start pedaling again."

With a shout of laughter, Danny moved to her and enfolded her in a gigantic bear hug, lifting her off the deck to swirl her around.

"Danny. Put me down. I'm getting dizzy."

Still laughing, Danny set her back on her feet and headed aft to raise the other sail. "Get that canvas up, sailor, and let's get out on the water. This kind of weather won't last much longer."

Perplexed, Tessa stared after Danny and muttered, "Aye, aye, sir."

They spent the afternoon sailing on the lake, enjoying the sunshine and the refreshing breezes glancing off the water. They worked the sails and the wheel together as if they'd been doing it all their lives. Tessa couldn't remember a time she'd been more relaxed. She glanced over at Danny, and at that moment he turned his head to look at her. Their gazes held, both of them unable to look away. Neither spoke. There was nothing to say. It was a time for connection, whether intended or not. There were no promises, no agreements and no arguments, just contentment. It was suddenly clear to both of them that the only thing to do was move forward and see where the road could lead. Finally Danny broke the silence, his voice husky and warm.

"What do you say, First Mate, are you hungry?"

Tessa tried to answer, but it took her a moment. She wet her lips, knowing that Danny was following every movement. "I'm starving."

"Then we'd better find a place to drop anchor for a while."

Tessa nodded and scanned the shoreline. "I don't know this lake at all, so you'll have to do the honors."

"There's a little inlet up ahead. We can drop anchor, find a stump and tie off there."

Together they adjusted the sheets to trim the boat so they could turn into the inlet and then strike the sails as they moved toward shore. Tessa looked around at the overhanging willow trees that hugged the shoreline. "It's beautiful here, like a little moment out of time."

Danny turned to her. "I think so, too. I used to come here as a kid. I had this old rowboat and outboard motor. I putt-putted that hunk of a hull all over this lake. This was one of my favorite places. I thought you might like it, too."

Tessa smiled at him. "I do. I like it very much. Did Laurie?"

For a moment Danny was silent. "I never brought Laurie here. I've only been here with one other woman." Then with a self-conscious nod, Danny jumped from the boat to the mossy bank.

Stunned by his confession, Tessa took her cue and threw him a tie-off line so the boat didn't drift. In a few minutes he'd completed his knot and was mounting the steps to the deck. For a moment Tessa couldn't move. She wasn't sure what was supposed to happen next, and from the look of him, neither was Danny. Finally she broke the silence, attempting to regain normalcy.

"So what do we have to eat—your favorite meal of peanut-butter sandwiches?"

Danny shook his head. "Oh, ye of little faith. Now, just sit back and relax. We have something much better than plain old peanut butter."

With a disbelieving look, Tessa asked, "And that would be?"

"A chef never tells," Danny said as he disappeared into the galley to locate the picnic basket he'd brought. A few minutes later he emerged with the basket in one hand and a small folding table in the other. Tessa rescued the table he gripped so precariously. "Thanks. The damn hinge was pinching my finger."

After looking around, Tessa decided to set the table where the aft bench met the port side bench in an L-shape. "How's this?"

"Excellent." He set the basket to the side before opening it with a flourish. He proceeded to set the small table with silverware and two china plates. Then he unearthed crystal wineglasses from the depths of the basket.

Tessa was impressed as she stared at the place settings. "I don't believe this. I expected plastic cutlery and paper plates."

Danny just grinned and presented a bottle of champagne, which he uncorked with as much drama as possible before pouring the liquid into their glasses. He held up his goblet. "A toast. Here's to a lovely day and an even lovelier companion."

"And to a beautiful restoration," Tessa said, nodding at the sailboat before touching her glass to his. "Cheers, Captain."

"Cheers, First Mate."

After their first sip, Tessa asked. "Okay, now I'm curious. What else is in that basket?"

Danny placed his glass on the table and rooted around inside before withdrawing a few plates covered with aluminum wrapping. "Hard-boiled eggs, celery with Cheez Whiz and carrots are our appetizer. For dessert we have strawberries and chocolate-and-cream pastries. And for the main course, the pièce de résistance—drum roll, please…" He whipped the aluminum foil from the plate. "Voilà!"

Tessa stared for a moment before fixing an accusing eye on Danny. "Those are peanut-butter sandwiches."

"These are peanut-butter, blackberry preserves and banana sandwiches on special-occasion bakery bread with the crusts cut off—much more elaborate than the everyday common-variety peanut-butter sandwich." He placed the sandwich on her plate as grandly as if he'd been serving Queen Elizabeth. "This 'Super-Duper Santori Special' is an old family recipe made especially for your enjoyment."

Tessa stared at the concoction on her plate, then raised her gaze to meet Danny's humorous one. "You are…" She started giggling like a little girl. "Words fail me."

With a grin, Danny nudged her plate toward her. "How about *eat up?*"

Nodding, Tessa did just that. After a few minutes of silence, a chagrined Danny mumbled, "I might have used too much peanut butter."

Tessa took a drink of champagne before she could unstick her lips to answer him. "I don't know what makes you think that."

Danny reached for his own drink to take a big gulp, then refilled their glasses. "How about some celery to clear the palate?"

"Quitter," Tessa said, taking another bite of her sandwich.

Not to be outdone, Danny took a bite and attempted to respond with a mush-mouthed comment of his own. "Can't refuse a challenge."

Finally they both gave up and reached for the strawberries and the chocolate-and-cream pastries, better known as Oreo cookies. Leaning back against the seat cushions, Tessa closed her eyes and inhaled deeply. "This is the life. I'm so relaxed I might slide right off this bench."

"It gets better."

Tessa opened one eye. "Impossible."

Danny dipped a strawberry in champagne and popped it into her mouth. "How's that?"

"Mmm," Tessa said, licking the juice from her lips. "Heavenly." She couldn't remember when she'd last been able to stay still and listen to the sounds around her, content to smell the air and feel the soft sunlight on her face. The table screeched on the deck as Danny shoved it away, but she still didn't move, knowing this was the moment she and Danny had been dancing around all afternoon.

She sighed, but Danny's lips caught her sigh as they descended onto hers. Her eyelashes fluttered in response, but it was too much effort to lift her lids. Instead she relaxed more, enjoying the pressure of Danny's mouth. It was soft and questing, drawing a response from her without conscious will, just need. Tessa let Danny take the glass from her hand, then raised her arms to rest her hands on his shoulders as she deepened the kiss, slipping her tongue inside his mouth to meet his. With a soft moan, Danny grabbed her forearms to fasten them around his neck while he enfolded Tessa in his arms in return.

"Tessa," he said, his voice low and husky. "Ah, Tessa. You are so sweet. Sweeter than I imagined. I want to taste and taste."

Tessa pressed closer, lifting her lips to say, "It's been such a long time."

"For me, too, sweetheart. For me, too."

He pulled her over onto his lap and proceeded to rain insistent pulsating kisses on her face, her lips, her neck, the tender area behind her ears, and all the while his hands were exploring her body, learning her shape, her scent, which resembled summer flowers, and the feel of her in his arms. His hand crept under her top, skimming over her silky skin until he reached the sweet curve of her breast. Tessa groaned and pressed herself more fully into his palm.

"Touch me," she whispered. "Please, touch me."

"Don't worry," Danny whispered back. "I couldn't stop myself even if I wanted to." He struggled to unsnap her bra one-handed, which took some doing, since it snapped in the back. With a final frustrated growl he released the hooks and pushed her top up so he could reach his prize, filling his hands with her before tasting her flesh, sucking her nipple into his mouth then laving it with his tongue before repeating the same caress on the other side.

"God, you're beautiful, like a classic statue, but warm—"

"Not warm, hot," Tessa whispered, smiling as she worked impatiently at the buttons on his shirt so she could touch his chest, from the soft spread of curls that arrowed down to his six-pack abs to his nipples standing out in relief from the sculpted muscles. She spread the shirt and leaned forward to stroke him with her hands, lips and tongue. His warm masculine scent went to her head faster than the intoxicating whiff of sweet roses in the heavy heat of midsummer.

Tessa wriggled closer to press against his chest. As their flesh met, Danny lifted her and laid her on the bench next to him, following her down to cover her body. Both of them tried to get closer as curves met angles, softness met hardness; both were caught in the joy of exploring, learning, feeling, teasing the way lovers do to extend the final moment of satisfaction.

"Danny, oh Danny…"

"Tessa" was all he said in response, his voice raspy with need. For the next few minutes the sounds of nature at its most contented were echoed by the groans of desire from Tessa and Danny as they moved toward fulfillment.

As Danny's hands slid her zipper down then moved to spread her thighs, he pressed rhythmically to heighten her pleasure. Tessa was almost passing out with feeling when she gasped, "Danny, Danny, tell me the truth. Tell me you've never brought Connie here?"

Danny raised his head from the grand tour of Tessa's body on his way to his final destination. "Who?"

"Connie." Tessa had no idea where the question had come from or why she had asked it during such an intimate time when her body was aching for satisfaction. Was she jealous? Was that it? Had her secret desire for Danny eliminated her caution?

Eyes unfocused with passion, Danny kissed her, a deep, soul-searing kiss that almost tore Tessa apart. "Forget Connie."

"Okay, but…" Now that she'd asked, she had to know. "Danny, you said you've been here with one other woman. I have to know if it was Connie so I know if what's happening between us could be as real as I think it is." Tessa might as well have had a mischievous imp sitting on her shoulder, urging her on in the wrong direction.

With a frustrated scowl, Danny levered away from her and almost fell off the bench before catching himself. "Did anyone ever tell you that for such an opinionated, sexy woman, you talk too much?"

At Danny's response, Tessa's hungry passion went from full boil to simmer. She raised herself onto her elbows. "Is there some reason you don't want to talk about her?"

"Hell, yes. I'm trying to make love to you."

"I know. That's why I have to know about her." At Danny's annoyed curse, Tessa wasn't sure whether to laugh or cry. Why did she need reassurance that she was different from the other woman he'd brought here, that their relationship was different, that she was special and not one of the crowd? Did this attitude come from her husband's many affairs, so she was attempting romantic self-sabotage with someone new?

Danny sat up, his face a study in exasperated frustration. He buttoned his shirt, buttoning it wrong before swearing and ripping it open again so buttons were flying like assault bullets. "The woman was my dog, Trixie. Connie is Laurie's great-aunt. She's seventy-two years old and recovering from a hip operation."

Tessa jerked to a sitting position. "What? For God's sake, why didn't you say so? Why pretend it was a hot date?"

"What did you expect me to do when you're running around flaunting your boyfriends in my face?"

"I wasn't flaunting. And it was just one boy…uh, man. And he was—" Tessa stopped, unsure whether to admit her own deception. "He was a blind date that Rhonda set me up with."

"What? Why?"

"I didn't want to get romantically involved with you."

"Didn't or don't?"

That was the real question that Tessa needed to answer to herself, although she already had a suspicion, but she was afraid to admit it. Instead she tried to change the subject, but Danny wouldn't let her.

"I asked you a question, Tessa."

"I can't answer it, Danny. I don't know what I'm feeling now. I can't…"

"A minute ago you sure could have, and so could I." Danny grasped her shoulders. "Look, I haven't been involved with anyone since Laurie died three years ago. God knows if I had been it wouldn't have been someone like you." At Tessa's outraged expression, he backtracked. "That came out wrong. I only mean, I thought it would be somebody who could put me first."

Tessa stiffened before swinging her legs to the deck, attempting to fasten her bra and make herself tidy. "That is an archaic attitude."

"I'm not denying it. But let's face it, what I do is very demanding, a lot more important than potting plants. My job has a lot of responsibility. I never know what I'm walking into when I leave my house or even if I'll be back, so I have to be sure that the woman in my life is—"

Tessa reared back, scooting across the bench. "How... how...dare you! Who are you to tell me what's important? You save lives and property, but I bring beauty into people's lives. I add to the environment. I—oh, forget it. I don't know why I'm even trying to explain, not when you've just made it clear what you've always been thinking." She started to get up, but was stopped by his hand on her arm.

"No, wait, Tessa. I didn't mean that exactly the way I said it. Sometimes I say things that..." He grabbed his hair and yanked, his frustration evident in every muscle of his body. "Forget that. What I'm thinking was very clear to you a few minutes ago." He glanced down at his visible erection. "It still is. Or it should be."

"That was sex, pure and simple. You don't have to think to have sex. It's a programmed response, like a bee knowing she has to collect pollen so she can make honey to feed the young."

"I'm not a bee and you sure as hell aren't as sweet as honey."

Eyes narrowed, Tessa stood up. "You know what, Danny Santori, you aren't a Neanderthal—you're more like a prehistoric worm."

With a haughty head toss she stood, but groaned when she realized she couldn't go anywhere. She was standing on a sailboat in a secluded inlet made for romance. In order to make a dignified exit she would have to sail back to the dock, ride back in the car and leave from his house. That would teach her to have an argument on a boat in the middle of a lake. All she wanted to do now was find a hole and hide so she could sob herself to sleep. If only she had kept her mouth shut, things might have been different. If only Danny had kept his mouth shut, things might have been different. She wasn't the only one who talked too much.

"Tessa," Danny said, walking over to touch her shoulders. "Let's sit down so we can talk about this like two rational adults."

"I don't want to talk." Tessa knew she sounded like a hurt child, but she couldn't help it.

His hands slipped down her arm. "Okay, we won't talk, then."

Tessa hunched her shoulders and moved away. "We aren't doing that, either. I want to go back. It's getting late and I have work to do."

Danny watched as Tessa walked to the steps, leaped onto the bank and furiously began untying the line holding them stationary while he wondered what in the hell had happened.

One minute he was in paradise and the next the serpent was gnawing on his insides. He ducked to avoid the line Tessa pitched in his direction. From the look on her face she was considering throwing the tree stump, too, but she resisted, climbing the stairs to the deck instead. Deciding retreat was the wisest course of action, Danny busied himself starting the motor so he could back from the inlet. Once on the water, he considered raising the sails, but one look at Tessa standing near the scene of almost sexual bliss changed his mind. He kept the motor running, skimming over the water so that they reached the dock in record time.

The ride home was quiet, with his comments being answered in abrupt sentences. Finally he gave up. Danny pulled into his driveway, but hadn't completely stopped when Tessa opened the car door.

"If you'll excuse me, I'll get back to my little pots of flowers."

He stepped hard on the brake as she scrambled from the seat. "Tessa—"

"Thank you. I had a lovely time." Her polite voice resembled a child thanking a hated relative for a crummy gift.

"Uh, okay, uh…thanks for coming." He got out of the car, too, waving toward the backyard. "Make sure you turn on the work lights so you can see back there. It's getting dark."

"I'm not an idiot, Danny," Tessa snapped.

Danny shrugged. "I was just trying to…" He hesitated for a minute, then removed the picnic basket and walked to the house. "I'm on duty tomorrow."

"I remember. My memory is excellent," Tessa answered as she stalked over to the walk leading to the backyard.

Danny was left staring after her, remembering the feel of her in his arms, wondering how something so wonderful had gone so wrong. *Women are so damn irrational.*

He defended himself—Tessa had started it. She was the one who had broken the mood by mentioning Connie. Who could think about another person at a time like that? The only thing he'd been thinking about was Tessa. But why in hell couldn't he have kept his mouth shut? He could have gotten the mood back. He could have—

Then he remembered his impulsive comment about their work, replaying it in his mind. After the fact, his statements sounded condescending. No wonder Tessa had lost her temper. The best thing he could do now was back off and leave her alone, even if the thought was killing him.

In the backyard, Tessa was thinking the same thing. She'd been so determined not to get involved that she hadn't been prepared. She hadn't been prepared to fall in love with Danny Santori. But she had.

More than that, she hadn't the faintest idea what to do next.

Chapter Ten

A loud pounding on the door woke Danny at five the next morning, a half hour before he had to get up to go to work. Swearing under his breath, he threw back the covers and padded to the front door, wearing nothing but a pair of jockey shorts and athletic socks. He was stunned to see a tousle-haired Tessa dressed in one of his old flannel shirts and leggings coming from the living room to see what the racket was about. After a puzzled look at her, he turned his attention to the pounding on his front door.

"All right, already," he muttered, opening the door to find himself facing a tall, handsome, annoyed man with Eric and Josie yawning beside him.

"Where is my wife?"

"Your what?"

"My wife, Tessa."

At his voice, Tessa darted around the door to stand next to Danny. "Colin, for heaven's sake, what are you doing here?"

"Collecting my wife—"

"Ex-wife."

Colin ignored her comment. "You're supposed to be home with our children in the morning."

"Mommy," Josie said, rubbing her eyes, "can we come in? I'm sleepy."

"Of course, honey." Tessa held the screen door open for Josie and Eric. "Go on upstairs to your beds, kids. Pancakes later this morning."

Danny watched as Tessa's children trailed up the stairs before turning his attention back to Colin. Tessa got to him first, however.

"What are you doing *here?* You said you were bringing the kids back this morning."

"It is morning and I have to catch a plane, which you would have known if you'd been home to hear that my plans have changed. I have to go back to Chicago immediately."

"I see. The company is going to fall apart without you, I suppose?"

"No, my fiancée has a difficulty that I have to take care of."

"Your what?" With a small encouraging squeeze, Danny's hands on her shoulder reassured a shocked Tessa of his support.

"You're engaged?" Danny asked.

Colin looked directly at him, then back at Tessa. "I don't know what is going on here, but I would like to speak to my…to Tessa in private."

Danny looked down at Tessa. "Are you okay with that?"

"Yes, go back to bed, Danny."

Danny grinned a wolfish grin. All his protective instincts had come to the fore as soon as Colin announced his relationship to Tessa, and he said the first thing that came to his mind. "I'm up now, sweetheart. I'll start the coffee and then I'm going to take a shower. You can join me when you finish here."

Obviously still off balance from Colin's news, Tessa paid no attention to what he said and gave Danny a little shove toward the kitchen. "Fine, go."

Danny headed off, but darted through the dining-room

arch instead. He didn't feel remotely guilty for listening to their conversation.

"Would you like to come in?" Tessa asked.

"No, thank you. Would you come out here…please?"

The door banged as Tessa stepped outside. "What is this all about? First you show up unannounced to see the kids this week instead of next week after not seeing them for months, and then you're banging on the door at 5:00 a.m."

"I came to tell the kids about their new stepmother and her desire to have them at the wedding. I'm banging on the door this morning because the mother of my children is not at her condo, but is instead sleeping with some…some…"

"Watch it, Colin," Tessa warned. "We aren't married anymore. Where I sleep or whom I sleep with is no longer your concern."

"It is when my children are involved."

"It's a shame you didn't think about that when we were married."

"Tessa…" Colin stared at her for a minute. "Look, I don't want to rehash our marriage on the porch, so can we—"

"Colin, Danny is a firefighter and we have an arrangement. I stay at his house when he's working and in return Josie and Eric stay here when I am."

Colin sent her a thoughtful look. "So you're living with him?"

"No, I'm not. But if I was living with Danny it's no longer your concern. You just said you're marrying someone else."

"My children…"

"*Our* children. *Our.* It takes two, remember? You just couldn't remember whom you were doing it with half the time. I suppose you're marrying Brandy, that perky little blonde assistant you were seeing before our divorce, the one you took to the Bahamas this summer?"

"No, I'm not marrying Brandy. And Brandy no longer

works for me. That's why I was trying to call you a few months ago to tell you." Colin's voice was defensive.

"Why would you tell me that? It wouldn't have made any difference to me."

"I don't know why I wanted to tell you." Colin looked almost guilty, but recovered his usual swagger. "But it doesn't matter anymore. I met someone new."

"Oh? What a surprise," Tessa said, the sarcasm dripping from her voice.

"I'm marrying Lucia del Reviente."

"What? You mean that Brazilian model for that lingerie company? Isn't she like twelve or something?"

Colin scowled. "That's not funny, Tessa. She's twenty, not twelve. We met at a photo shoot."

"Well, well, haven't you come up in the world. If business is so good that you can afford to pay a model like that, then you can increase my monthly child support, too, since you recently found some extra investments so you could start a trust for each child."

Colin flushed. "I'll speak to my lawyer about providing a bit more."

"Good." Tessa folded her arms and leaned back against the door. "Congratulations, Colin. I'll bet Lucia will be a great hit with the men at corporate parties. I can't see her with all the wives, though. How did you convince her to give up her career?"

"I didn't try. She is going to continue modeling, then plans to start a fashion line. Naturally I'll be involved with that, too."

"So this Lucia having a career is fine, but my having one was a problem?"

From the stuffy sound of Colin's answer, Danny figured his nose had stopped up or else he was living dangerously with his response. It made Danny realize again just how arrogant his comments had sounded the day before on the boat. No wonder Tessa was so determined to succeed on her own. The next thing he heard was a car door slam and the creak of the front door as Tessa came back inside. He peered out of the dining room before stepping into the hallway.

"Tessa? Baby, are you all right?"

Tessa jumped. "Danny, stop creeping up on me, and don't call me baby. I hate that." She stared at him for a long moment before adding, "I suppose you overheard my conversation?"

Danny nodded as he strolled over to her. "He's getting married? Are you okay with that?"

"I have no feelings left for Colin. Haven't for a long time. Colin really wasn't around a great deal. He was working or traveling or amusing himself elsewhere." She heaved an anxious sigh. "I have to talk to my children. I hope they're all right with this."

"They're good kids, Tessa. You've done a great job with them."

"Thank you."

"I mean every word of it. They're really special."

"You aren't going to distract me by talking about my children." Tessa placed her hands on her hips, drawing Danny's attention back to her lack of clothing. "Why did you try to make Colin think we're involved?"

"Tessa, we are involved. We're just having problems working out the details." Before Tessa could reply he changed the subject. "What are you doing here anyway? I thought you left last night."

"I did, but…my condo seemed empty all of a sudden, so I drove over here about 2:00 a.m. Since you're on shift today, I would have had to come back anyway. I planned to ask Rhonda to drop off the kids after Colin brought them back."

"And my shirt?" Danny asked, indicating the flannel covering her luscious body. "Which looks a lot better on you than me, by the way."

Tessa blushed. "I was cold, and you'd left the shirt in the living room, so I—"

"Decided to sleep half-nude on my sofa?" He grinned. "Don't misunderstand—I'm not complaining."

Tessa attempted to be casual. "I'm not half-nude. I'm wearing a T-shirt and leggings underneath."

"I noticed. You look delicious all sleepy and rumpled."

"Um…thank you," she ventured, her cheeks flushing again.

With a laugh he dropped a kiss on her nose. "You look so cute when you're flustered."

"Stop flirting, Danny. We decided yesterday…"

Not ready to talk about yesterday, Danny changed the subject. "How did Colin know to come to my house?"

"Huh? Oh, my kids probably told him. They love it over here. We all think of it as a second home."

To Danny's delight, Tessa's blush deepened until she was as red as one of his fire engines. He decided to ignore that comment, too, because he didn't have time to deal with it properly either. "I have to get dressed if I'm going to get to work on time. Coffee is in the pot if you want some."

"Danny…"

He stopped on the stairs and turned to look at her. "What?"

"Thank you."

"For what? I didn't do anything."

"You stood up for me. I appreciate that, but you can't keep telling people that we are, have—well…" With a self-conscious expression Tessa muttered, "You know what I mean."

Danny was careful to hide his smile. "Let's table a discussion about us until after your holiday show. Then we can talk about what's next."

A relieved Tessa stared back at him. "You've got a deal."

BEFORE TESSA KNEW IT she was overseeing her final garden setup in Moonlight Gardens, a partially open pavilion surrounded by half and full walls. She prayed there would be no weather disasters to spoil the turnout at the show, especially since a portion of her display was exposed to the elements. So far there had been no snow to add to the holiday feeling, but the weather was crispy clear and the sky was an intense blue.

Tessa and her helpers had already erected the basic garden structure. Now she needed to flesh it out. She nodded at Danny and the children, who were bringing in a few final trees and flowers.

"Tessa, the kids and I have to take off," Danny said. "I've got tons of paperwork to do because the chief is out of town. I have to do my best work, since I'm in charge."

Tessa smiled. "You'd do your best even if you weren't in charge, Danny."

"You got me there. Is there anything else you need before I go?"

Looking around, Tessa replied absently, "I don't think so."

Danny indicated Alison on her knees in front of the display. "If it's okay, Alison wants to stay."

"Great. I couldn't do without her."

Danny handed her a paper bag. "Emma made your lunch."

Tessa grinned. "Peanut-butter sandwiches?"

Danny managed to answer with a straight face. "With blackberry jelly. How did you guess?"

"I'm a mind reader."

With a wink and a smile, Danny commented, "That might come in handy someday, sweetheart."

"Danny," Tessa warned, knowing he wouldn't pay the slightest bit of attention to her, but would keep flirting with her whenever and wherever he liked.

His grin expanded. "We'll all see you later. Come on, kids,

time to let the gardeners get back to work." With a wave Danny and the kids left. Tessa returned to removing the contents from one of the boxes.

"Alison, where are the fairies?" she called.

"I'm right over here, darling," Barrett called.

Tessa glanced over her shoulder at the slight older gentleman standing in front of his own display across the aisle. She laughed. "Oh, be quiet, Barrett. You know I wasn't talking about you."

"I must say, Tessa, darling, that I do like what you're doing over there. It's very appealing and wonderfully romantic." Then he added with a sly twinkling smile, "I think it a perfect place for fairies to romp."

Tessa grinned back at him.

"I found them, Tessa," Alison called.

Tessa waved her over. "It was Alison's idea. Alison, this is Barrett. He's a competitor of mine."

"Nonsense, darling," Barrett said. "I have a floral shop. I don't do landscapes, except a few flower gardens for old friends like Mrs. Deerfield. I'd rather do weddings and party events. They're much more fun." Barrett turned to Alison. "I was just telling Tessa how much I love your idea of making a secret fairy garden. It's delightful, dear."

Alison blushed and ducked her head. "It was really Tessa, Mr. Barrett."

Barrett waved his hand. "No Mister is necessary. I only use Barrett."

"Alison is being shy, Barrett. It was her idea, not mine."

"Well, darlings, I'll leave you to fight it out. My bird-of-paradise plants have just arrived. You know, Tessa, we should discuss collaborating on a project. I think it would challenge both of us."

"Say the word, Barrett, and I'm there." Tessa watched him leave to fuss over his flowers.

"We'll have lunch, darling girl."

"He's funny," Alison commented, then she asked in a hesitant tone, "Tessa, would it be okay if some friends stopped by tonight to see what we're doing?"

"I guess so, as long as you're careful and don't disturb anything."

Alison's expression reverted to the sulky defensive one that Tessa hadn't seen for weeks. "I wouldn't do that."

After a quick glance at Alison, Tessa smiled, trying to restore the harmonious atmosphere they'd established over the past few weeks. "I know. So who's coming?"

"Tiffany and a few others."

"Tiffany? Queen bee Tiffany?"

Alison nodded. "Mmm-hmm...She's not as bad as I thought, as long as you follow..."

"Follow what? Her rules?" Tessa stared at Alison when she didn't answer. "So how's it going with that boy you like? Rob, is it?"

"I'm over Rob."

Tessa grinned. "Well, that was fast."

"He's so immature. He's only a freshman."

"So are you." Tessa went back to unpacking a box. "Is there someone more mature you're thinking about?"

"Maybe," Alison said in a teasing tone. "But you can't tell Dad."

"It's okay, you don't have to tell me."

"See, there's this guy. He's so...so..." The expression on Alison's face told Tessa all she needed to know about Alison's feelings.

"Pretty hot, huh?" Tessa asked, hiding a smile.

Alison turned red, but avoided answering. "He's a friend

of Tiffany's brother. He might come over tonight, too, if that's okay."

"Sure. Look…I'm supposed to leave for a while this evening to attend that event for the show participants, but I can stay and finish up here so you can pay more attention to Mr. Hottie if you want."

"That's dumb. You said you'd meet a lot of people at the event who could help your business."

"My business won't be worth anything if this display doesn't knock everyone's socks off."

"It will. Look at it so far." Alison turned and spread her arms. "It's great."

Tessa stopped pacing and took a good look at what they'd accomplished so far. She felt they'd nabbed the perfect place for their display. They were tucked into a corner of the pavilion not too far from the entrance for good consumer traffic, but they had the forest as a backdrop, which was perfect for the secret and secluded atmosphere she was trying to create.

The garden was as enclosed as they could make it to replicate a pleasure garden. After entering through the distressed door in an arbor covered with climbing roses, guests were invited to view the curved planting areas tucked next to the winding brick path that wove in and around the taller woodbine or honeysuckle, box shrubs, hawthorn, crabapple and cherry trees.

The seasons changed from spring bulbs of tulips, daffodils, windflowers and early old-fashioned scented roses to summer and fall plantings of herbs such as lavender, lemon balm, fennel, basil, rosemary and rue, their subtle hues offset by the colors of violets, pansies, myrtle, daisies and geraniums. Fall harvest displays of nuts, minipumpkins, squash, mums, more pansies and black-eyed Susans were followed by an area featuring grasses, red-fruited winterberry, more small trees and ground covers that created an artistic experience defined by texture, shape, outlines and hues. The entire winter section sparkled like a winter fairy tale. The highlight of the display was a small sleigh filled with pine boughs and frosted with a silver snow spray touched with golden sparkles and the brilliant red of poinsettias, plus holly and tiny mistletoe berries. The scent of pine, hot apple pie and hot chocolate wafted out to greet guests as they arrived to celebrate the winter holidays.

In each of the seasons fairy figures played, hid, smiled and invited guests to discover them as they frolicked beneath the leaves and flowers and hid behind the woody branches before emerging to stage a holiday event of their own on the mirror pond in the center of the winter landscape.

They worked the rest of the afternoon before Tessa straightened from arranging a bower of sweet petunias, zinnias and hollyhocks that formed another hiding place for the summer fairies. Glancing at her watch, she leaped to her feet. "Oh my God, look at the time. I have to take a shower, get dressed, and we still have things to do before the judging tomorrow evening." She looked around at the display. "Maybe I shouldn't go."

"Stop that. All the big things are finished. We only have finishing details." Alison handed over Tessa's tote bag and practically pushed her out of the garden. "If you don't hurry up, you'll miss the appetizers."

Tessa laughed as her stomach suddenly growled. "Well, I don't want to do that. I think I forgot to eat lunch."

A huge grin from Alison teased as she said, "You still have Emma's PB&J sandwich. The bread is kind of soggy from the jelly, but…"

Tessa laughed. "I'll pass, thanks. Okay, if you're sure everything is under control, I'll take off and be back later this evening." Tessa tossed her bag over her shoulder. "If you're ready to leave before I—"

"Go." Alison laughed, giving Tessa another push. "I won't leave before you come back."

"All right, I'll see you later."

TWO HOURS LATER Danny walked into a disaster. He and the kids had just arrived at the holiday display when he heard someone yell, "Don't let it spread. Put it out, dude!"

Telling Eric, Josie and the twins to stay by the entrance, Danny raced over to the sound of the panicked voice and the smell of smoke. He found a few teenage girls and boys trying to fade away from the scene of the crime, while his daughter was tackling a small fire in the cardboard boxes piled near the display. Danny pushed Alison out of the way and ordered, "Call it in."

He pointed at a teenage boy who had been trying to help Alison. "You, find a fire extinguisher."

"Yes, sir," the boy said, eyeing his fleeing friends. He ran to the nearest exit looking for the distinctive red canister. While he was gone, Danny took off his jacket and began beating the growing flames to smother them. Within minutes he heard the wail of a siren, and the boy reappeared with an extinguisher in his arms. Danny grabbed it and started spraying the fire. A crash indicated that the on-duty firemen had arrived, pushing their way through the double doors. The paramedics who routinely accompanied station calls followed them. Firemen in full uniform converged on the location of the fire, and quickly assessed the situation, which was under control.

"This the only flame?" Murphy, the first crewman asked, his alert glance sweeping the pavilion, noting the many displays that were making up the show.

Danny put down the canister and wiped his sweating brow with his forearm. "As far as I know it is. It had just started when I got here, but you'd better check the rest of the area to be certain."

"Already doing that. Lucky there aren't many people here at the moment. How'd it start?"

Danny eyed his daughter before answering. "Not sure yet."

Another voice yelled, "Hey, Santori, can't stay away from work, huh?"

Danny turned and stared at the tall young fireman. "Hey there, Jake. You're too late for this party."

Jake Doren laughed. "Things have been hopping tonight. This is our third call already. What the hell happened here?"

For the first time Danny was able to view his surroundings, and what he saw made his stomach sink to his feet. Flowers were trampled, one part of the fieldstone wall that Tessa had created had fallen down and it looked as if someone had crushed a small fairy cottage tucked under a spray of roses. "Oh, hell, Tessa can't see this display like this. She's been working on this project for over five weeks straight."

Jake waved to one of the other fireman and turned back to Danny. "We've got the all clear, Danny, but we need some answers for the report."

Danny took Jake aside. "I'll find out how it went down and let you know, okay?"

Jake looked from Danny to a shocked and miserable-looking Alison. "Yeah, okay, boss. We'll head back to the station."

"Jake, see if you can round up anyone off duty tonight, will you? I'm going to need help to put this back together before the show begins."

"I'll make some calls on the way to the truck and see who's around."

"Thanks, Jake. Beer and pizza is on me next week."

"I'll hold you to that, buddy." Jake strode toward the door, pulling a phone out of his pocket.

From the corner of his eye Danny saw Alison staring at the mess. "All right, young lady, perhaps you'd better tell me what happened here."

Before Alison could answer, Eric, Josie, Emma, Kevin and Kyle came running up, talking a mile a minute. Danny held up his hand. "Hold it. I can't hear myself think."

"Jeez, it looks like a bulldozer ran through here," Eric commented after looking around. "Mom's going to freak!"

"We're all going to help out and fix it up so that doesn't happen."

Josie sent him a very adult look. "She'll freak anyway. Mom does that sometimes."

Danny smiled. "Yes, I know. I've seen her in action." His smile faded when he caught sight of Alison now hovering close to the display, staring at the destruction. The teenage boy who had found the fire extinguisher had disappeared, leaving only Alison to face the music—whatever the music was.

"Kids, see if you can pick up those broken pots and flowers and throw them into the trash can while I talk to Alison." He crooked a finger at his oldest daughter and led her away from the display. "All right, spill it. What happened, young lady?"

Alison bit her lip and looked at the floor.

"Alison, answer me. Did this have anything to do with those kids who ran out when the fire started?"

"Those kids are my friends."

"Some friends," Danny said, the sarcasm in his voice blistering his daughter, who reacted defensively.

"They're some of the most popular kids in school and they came here because I asked them to come."

"So your 'friends' came and decided to trash the place?"

"It wasn't like that. They were screwing around, pushing each other and—"

"Why were they doing that? Did it have anything to do with the beer cans I found by the boxes? Were they drinking?"

Alison shrugged, her mouth set defiantly. "I guess so."

"How old are these 'friends' who split and left you to take all the blame?"

"The boys are juniors. They came with Tiffany and some other girls."

"Juniors who were drinking in a public place?"

"Yeah, I guess," Alison said with another shrug.

"'I guess'? You don't know?"

Alison muttered an incomprehensible reply.

"Alison, do you understand how serious this is? What this means to Tessa to have this show succeed?"

"Sure, I've been working with her, haven't I?"

"Don't get smart," Danny warned.

"Tessa said I could have friends stop by," Alison said, trying to justify her actions.

"Did she say it was okay to trash the place?"

"Dad," Alison wailed. "It was an accident."

"No, what happened was bad judgment on your part and on the part of your friends."

Alison gave him a sulky look. It was the attitude she'd been exhibiting since the summer, the one Tessa's patient influence and this project had helped erase. *So it's back to square one with this kid.* Not for the first time, Danny wished his wife were alive to handle his daughter, since he didn't think Tessa would be any help at all after she'd seen this mess.

"Did one of these 'friends' light a cigarette, then throw it in the box?"

"I guess so."

"Again, you guess so? Don't you know? Weren't you here?"

"Yes, sir, I was here."

Danny stared down at Alison, watching her face change

from defiant to childlike. "We'll discuss this later. There will be repercussions for not taking responsibility, Alison. Right now we have to start repairing this mess." He turned away to take stock of the display, anger rising again as he saw the amount of the damage.

"Daddy," Alison said in a small voice.

"What?" he snapped, his frustration fast reaching boiling.

"Nothing," she replied in a choking voice.

"Wait a minute, Alison." Danny stopped her as she began walking toward the display. "What is it?"

"I'm sorry," she whispered.

"I'm not the one you have to tell. You need to tell Tessa."

Alison shook her head. "I don't think I can face her, Daddy."

"You'll have to—that's what taking responsibility is all about."

Gnawing on her fingernails, Alison whispered, "She'll hate me."

Danny crossed his arms as he faced his daughter. "You should have thought about that earlier."

Alison sobbed, her misery breaking through. Danny relented enough to pull her close for a hug. "It's okay, honey. We're going to pull together and fix it."

She squeezed him so tightly he almost gasped. He slipped his handkerchief from his pocket and handed it to Alison. "Mop up—here comes Tessa." Her arms tightened instead as she heard the clip of Tessa's high heels hurrying toward them. One last squeeze and Alison stepped back from her father, ready to face Tessa's wrath.

"She'll hate me, Daddy," Alison said softly.

Tessa swept across the pavilion, her skirt swinging and high heels clicking on the concrete. "Danny, why didn't you tell me you were bringing the kids over here? I went to your house to pick them up and no one was home. I panicked,

imagining you had to take someone to the hospital or..."
Tessa jerked to a stop as she caught sight of her display.

"What...happened...to..." She couldn't speak, waving instead to the fairy garden.

"Tessa, there was an incident."

After a scared glance at her father, Alison stepped forward. "It's my fault, Tessa. I did it."

Tessa stared at her, the shock she felt pushing words from her mouth. "How could you do this? Do you hate me that much? I thought you and I were..." Tessa caught sight of Alison's stricken face and clamped her lips shut.

Alison gulped and said in a small voice, "I know I've been a brat and I'm sorry for that. I don't hate you. I'd never do something like this on purpose."

Danny smoothed his hands over Tessa's arms. Tessa looked up into his sympathetic eyes. "Give Alison a chance to explain, okay?"

Tessa nodded and Alison's words tumbled forth. "The kids I invited brought some friends and they had some beer and started clowning around, pushing and shoving, and the next thing...they had fallen into the display. Then, then...then...somebody lit a cigarette and tossed the match into some boxes and, and... Oh, Tessa, I'm so sorry. It's all my fault. Dad's right—I should have stopped them. I should have...I don't know, I should have done something. Can you ever forgive me for acting like a total wimp?" Alison started sobbing. "Please, Tessa. I'm going to fix it. You won't know anything happened."

After a long moment Tessa faced Alison, saying in an even voice, "I left you in charge. Do you know what that means?"

Alison gasped and the tears flowed faster. "I know. I screwed up, big-time."

"Yes, you did. You knew how important this display was to my future business."

"Yes, ma'am. But you said I could have some people come over to look."

"Look, not ruin." Tessa stared at Alison a moment longer, noticing the tears in her eyes but unable and truthfully unwilling to comfort her at the moment. Finally she pulled her gaze away and looked at Danny, then over to the other children, who were picking up some garden debris. Her control collapsed and she whispered, "We'll never fix this in time."

Danny's hand on her arm stopped her as she started to walk away. "Yes, we will. All of us are here to help. Tell us what to do."

Tessa sighed. "I think the kids should go home."

"Tessa, they really want to help right now. I'll get them home in a little while."

"I'm not sure if we can make it before the judges see it."

"Don't you give up on me, Tessa Doherty. You don't give up, remember? You're the woman who walked out on a cozy lifestyle because she wanted something for herself. Now is your chance. If you let a little obstacle like this stop you, then you're not the woman I think you are."

"A little obstacle," Tessa repeated before meeting his determined eyes, and then Alison's hopeful ones. She noticed the younger children bustling around the display picking up a few broken flowers. Standing a bit straighter, Tessa rubbed her forehead, trying to concentrate. Her jaw firmed and her eyes narrowed. "All right. All right, we'll give it our best shot. Alison, see if any of the fairies survived."

"Yes, ma'am," an eager Alison replied, dashing away her tears and then almost running over Emma in her rush to help.

"Danny, maybe the rest of the kids could finish clearing the small debris so I can make a better assessment of the damage. After that we have to rebuild the wall, fix the trellis and the garden statues…." She swallowed a sob as she thrust her hands through her hair. "Oh my God, Danny, how am I going to get this all done before tomorrow evening? I'll never make it. I'll probably have to locate flowers again and...maybe I should—"

"Steady, sweetheart. Take a breath. You're not a quitter. You're a strong, capable woman who loves a challenge. Besides, you've got me and I've got reinforcements coming." He jerked his thumb toward the door, where several people were entering. "Over here, guys."

Tessa turned to watch as a tall, lithe red-haired woman in her twenties strode toward them. Beth Simmons and three guys accompanied her.

Danny hugged the small blonde woman. "Hey, cutie, how's your new fiancé?"

"Lucky to have me." Beth grinned back at Danny before glancing at Tessa. "Hi again, Tessa. Rhonda couldn't come to help. She just got called in to the E.R. The place is a madhouse tonight." Beth poked the tall redhead and nodded toward Tessa.

"What?" The redhead frowned before getting Beth's meaning. "Oh, sorry, I'm CJ Doren, and this motley crew," CJ said, pointing to the men, "had nothing to do tonight so my twin brother, Jake, told me to bring them along."

Tessa smiled at the group. "Thanks for coming. I really appreciate it."

CJ turned a curious look onto the garden display. "Looks like one of our engines flattened the place, Danny."

Danny's smile hardened. "Nope, it was teenagers."

"Just as destructive," CJ commented. "Where do we start?"

Turning to Tessa, Danny said, "Tell us what you need, boss."

After taking a deep breath, Tessa started giving orders. "Let's start by rebuilding the wall, then doing something with the trellis. It looks as if it's broken, but we can probably glue or tape it and drape the wisteria over it to hide the repair. Then we can fix anything else broken. I need help inventorying the smashed blooms so I can focus on what flowers I need to replace. Also, if there are any bushes with broken branches we'll need to pull them out and replace them. At least the brick path looks undamaged, but I have a feeling the sundial has seen better days."

Without waiting for any other instructions the five new recruits pitched in, working as if they'd been working together their entire lives. When she commented on this to Danny he told her, "Except for Beth, the rest of us are in the fire department. Our lives depend on teamwork. That's what we do. We pitch in when there's a need. It gets to be a habit."

Tessa smiled. "It's a great habit to develop."

"That's what I keep telling you. You and I could make one hell of a team if we wanted to."

Tessa stared at him for a long moment, then walked away from the display so they wouldn't be overheard. She whispered, "Danny, you're impossible. One minute it's no good and the next everything is full speed ahead. I never quite know where I am with you."

"It goes both ways, sweetheart."

"You said we'd wait to talk about us until after the show. I can't even think about this until then. I've invested most of my spare cash in this project. I have to make it a success."

"Don't worry about the display. It's going to be great."

Suddenly Beth yelled from the other end of the display, snaring Tessa's attention. "CJ, don't move." CJ froze. "Back up, CJ...oops, slowly so you don't step on one of the fairies."

CJ glared at her friend. "Jeez, Beth, is that why you scared me out of three years' growth? 'Cause I might step on a fairy? I'm an EMT—I can fix the damn fairy."

Tessa laughed, the first lifting of her spirits she'd had since she walked in to see her work in ruins. She glanced back at Danny. "I thought CJ was a fireman."

"She was…is…but she's working on her paramedic courses. She decided there was something about seeing men helpless in the back of an ambulance that moved her."

"I see her point." Tessa grinned.

"I thought you might," Danny said with a wry expression. "Why don't you get your notebook and do a walk-through to see what new flowers or materials you need? We can go out first thing tomorrow morning and pick up what's been ruined. Don't worry," he said as Tessa's face took on a worried look. "I'm paying for it. My daughter was responsible."

"But—"

"Don't argue with me, Tessa. I'm paying, and that's final."

After a moment Tessa agreed. "Okay, but I consider it a loan."

"No, it's not. It's what teamwork is all about. You need something and I can provide it. Regardless, it gets done. I know you want to make it on your own, but it's not always possible to be a one-man band. Everyone needs someone in their corner. You have to learn to be more gracious about accepting help."

"I…you're right. Thank you, Danny."

With a brisk nod, Danny replied, "You're welcome."

"I'm not trying to be difficult. It's just that I grew up seeing my mother's needs subjugated to someone else. My marriage was the same way, so I think I'm going to the other extreme. But sometimes I never feel like I do anything right regardless of how hard I try."

"After the judging tomorrow—" Danny rose to his feet "—I don't think that will be a problem. By the time we finish no one will ever know your fairy garden isn't as original as the designer. I expect good things from you, Tessa Doherty."

Ignoring the curious glances from those who were working

on the display, Danny reached over to cup the back of her neck and draw her toward him. He dropped a quick kiss on her lips before swatting her bottom. "Let's get back to work."

Somehow Tessa, Danny, Alison and the rest of the crew managed to put the display back together in record time. As the judges came by the next night for their last look at the exhibits before making their final decisions, Danny and the kids were there in the audience for moral support. All except Alison. Tessa had insisted Alison stand with her in the display.

"After all," Tessa had said, "it was your idea. You deserve to be there, too."

Alison had been overwhelmed, protesting that she'd almost ruined the entire thing, but Tessa had told her that the most important thing was standing up and telling the truth and helping to fix the problem. So as Tessa stood, clad in silver, before the winter season in her display, Alison stood next to her, dressed in a holly-berry-red dress that they'd made time to find just that afternoon.

Tessa held Alison's hand as the judges strolled through the exhibit. Mostly the judges presented stone faces, but a few of them seemed very taken with the cunning use of the fairies cavorting among the seasons. To Tessa's surprise, one of the judges whispered as she was leaving, "Absolutely charming, Ms. Doherty. Perhaps after the judges' announcements you and I could talk about a personal project I have in mind?"

"Oh, my gosh, Tessa," Alison whispered. "Did you hear that?"

"You heard it, too? Thank God. I thought it was my wishful thinking."

Alison threw her arms around Tessa. "This is the best night of my life. Thank you, Tessa."

"No," Tessa said, pulling the young girl closer. "Thank you. I couldn't have done this without you."

Alison's eyes lit up. "Really?"

Tessa kissed Alison's forehead. "Absolutely."

Alison looked at the display, then back at Tessa. "Um, do you think I could continue working with you sometimes?"

"I couldn't do without you, Alison."

After that exchange, hearing Tessa Doherty, Living Lifestyles, announced as the winner of an honorable mention for the Most Creative Display by a New Artist was the icing on the cake. Now, if she could get a few more clients from the show so she could get through the winter months, her life might finally be heading in the right direction.

Then her only problem would be Danny. Danny and how she felt about him. Danny and how he felt about her. She had feelings for him. He had feelings for her, too, she knew. But she wondered...

Are feelings enough to build a successful future?

Chapter Eleven

Naturally the unseasonable good weather came to an end after the show, which was immediately followed by wind, cold and snow flurries. On one crisp starry night Tessa stopped by Danny's house to pick up her kids. With the engine running she honked the horn, only to have Danny appear and open her car door.

"Hey, you're just in time. Dinner is almost ready."

"That's not necessary, Danny. I have tonight totally free, so I thought I'd go home and give the kids dinner before I curl up on the sofa."

"Please stay. The kids helped with dinner. They'd be disappointed if you left. And I'd be highly insulted."

Tessa chuckled. "We wouldn't want that, would we?" She allowed Danny to usher her out of the car and into the house.

After a boisterous meal of stick-to-your-ribs beef stew—which Danny had proudly cooked in the Crock-Pot—cheese biscuits, which he'd bought, plus cookies made from a mix by the kids, Danny sent the older kids off to finish their homework while he and Tessa put Emma to bed. Finally Danny suggested they bundle up and take their coffee onto the porch. As always, they gravitated to the porch swing.

Tessa sighed as she leaned back. "I'm going to miss this swing."

"Why? Where are you going?"

"I'm getting a lot more business since the show, and I have some other opportunities with Barrett that I'd never considered. You know Barrett, don't you?"

"The silver-haired dude in the expensive suit who had that froufrou display next to you?"

Even a hard-of-hearing amoeba couldn't have missed the disapproval in Tessa's voice as she answered, "The distinguished gentleman with that very artistic display of flowers and art, you mean? Yes, that's Barrett."

Danny held up his hand for peace. "I didn't mean that the way it sounded. I'm not the most artistic guy, so I didn't know how to describe it. I liked Barrett. What about him?"

"We had lunch last week and started talking about some projects we can do together. Since he's a florist, he'd do the flower-arrangement design, but I'd design the environment around it. That started me thinking it might be good to add in party design and planning to my business services. What do you think?"

Danny sipped his coffee. "Sure, that sounds okay. But I don't really get what you mean by that."

"Barrett has this client who is looking to transform a living and dining room into a winter wonderland for Christmas. I'd create the wonderland look of the entire area, placing flowers and plants to frame the theme. Barrett would do all the floral arrangements for the table and for other areas where a display was needed, in addition to creating personal flowers for the guests of honor, things like that."

"It sounds as if that type of thing will take a lot more of your time. We haven't seen much of each other since the show as it is. I thought you'd been avoiding me."

Tessa took a gulp of her coffee. "No, I'm working more now. And it's not as if you've been hugging the sofa, either. When you're not on duty, the kids told me you're bringing work home."

"If you work hard enough you get ahead. At least, that's what was drilled into me as a kid. We just got a good government resource grant, so I've been working with Mike on the curriculum and the advanced training procedures."

"That sounds interesting. What's invol—" Tessa began, breaking off with a yawn so wide that Danny was afraid her jaw would break. "You'll have to tell me later. I'm whipped. I'd better take my kids home so I can go to sleep."

"Stay." Danny took Tessa's mug and placed it on the table beside his. "It will give us some more time together."

"That's not a good idea. You're on duty tomorrow so we both have to get up early and— Stop that."

"I love the way your mouth trembles when you say no, but don't want to," Danny said, continuing to nuzzle her neck.

"What is it you think I want?"

"You want the same thing I do."

"I'm not sure about that. I can't stay at home like Laurie did and not have a career. I'm sorry if that's what you want, but—"

"That isn't what I want. I'm talking about working as a team. In a team everyone pulls their weight. Laurie and I shared equally."

"Yes, she stayed home and you went to work."

"That's what made sense for us," Danny said with a casual shrug.

"It doesn't make sense for me."

"Why should it? You're not Laurie."

Tessa's mouth dropped open as she stared at him, suddenly infuriated by his reasonable tone. "That's what I've been telling you. God, you drive me so crazy I could just…just…" She yanked off her hat and threw it at him, delighting him so much that he reached for her and drew her into a mind-blowing kiss.

"Danny." Tessa sighed before making a halfhearted effort to move away. "You're pushing me and I don't want to be pushed anymore."

"Woman, you would drive a saint to hell." He shoved his way upright from the swing, then thrust his hands into his hair. "Damn it, Tessa, I think I'm in love with you. Why can't you understand that? How many more ways do I have to say it?"

Tessa leaped to her feet and tossed his tone right back to him. "You have to say it until you get it right for both of us. And I think I'm in love with you, too, so don't shout at me like the fireman in charge of the situation."

As the realization of what they'd both said hit them they dropped back onto the swing. Glancing once at each other, they couldn't hold the gaze. They both looked away. For a few minutes the only noise was the rattling rustle of the leaves still on the ground and the scurrying of a squirrel on night patrol.

"What did you say?" Tessa ventured.

Danny rubbed his chin. "I'm not quite sure."

"You said you think you might be in love with me. Don't deny it."

"I'm not denying it. I'm just surprised it popped out."

"Did you mean it?"

Danny was quick to reply, "Did you?"

After one searching glance, Tessa stared at her feet. "I...yes, I think so."

"You think so?"

"I didn't plan to say it, either. It slipped out."

There was another long silence while they both processed their statements. Danny broke the silence. "So if we love each other, what's the problem with our being together?"

"I keep telling you, we're the problem. You and me. What

we want. What we need. I need freedom and respect for what I want to accomplish. I need to reach out and try things I've never done before."

"And marriage to me would prevent that?"

"Who's talking about marriage?"

Danny hesitated, a stunned look on his face. "I, uh, I guess I was…uh, am. Me, I think."

"I just admitted to myself very recently that I was in love with you…but marriage. I don't know…"

"I don't, either. But I do know that I haven't been involved with anyone like this since Laurie. I've avoided involvement. I figured I had enough responsibility with my kids and career. I didn't expect to meet anyone I'd feel this way about. So to me the next logical step is marriage. We sure as hell can't live in sin with six kids running around."

Tessa was silent, not sure what to say. No, that wasn't true. She wanted to say *yes*. Then she would throw her arms around him and never let him go. He was a very special man, but… Frustrated, she slapped her hand on the arm of the swing. "Why do you do this, Danny?"

"Do what?"

"Bring up things like this without warning."

"How am I supposed to warn you? Hire a flock of doves? Throw flowers at your feet? Wave a flag?"

"I don't know, but you could have prepared me somehow."

He dropped his head back. "Tessa Doherty, you drive me crazy."

She lifted her chin. "In that case I'm surprised you want to marry me."

"It surprises the hell out of me, too," Danny said.

Glaring at each other, they fell silent again.

Tessa peeped at him from under her lashes. "I really have to think about this."

Looking a bit hurt, Danny said, "Fine—you do that. I'll think about it, too."

"You have to think about it?"

"You're not the only one who's scared."

Tessa jumped into denial mode. "I'm not scared. I'm being deliberate. There are many things to consider."

"Bull," Danny snorted. "You're terrified. That's what this 'freedom to go my way' excuse of yours is about. What it's always been about."

"That's not true."

"It is true. You're afraid to take a risk."

"I'm taking a risk," Tessa stated. "I left Colin, I started a business, I…"

Danny shook his head. "You run like hell if anyone gets too close to your heart."

"My kids are close to my heart, and so are yours. Then there's my work, my—"

Turning to face her, Danny said, "None of that counts. Until you open yourself enough to let a man in, too, into your heart, your mind, your body—the rest is just responsibility. That's what this is really about. You're afraid of yourself, of how I make you feel."

Tessa jumped on one statement. "You're wrong. I'm not afraid. I am responsible for my life now, for Eric and Josie, for…" At Danny's skeptical look she trailed off. "I need some space here. Maybe we should make other arrangements for the children for a while. Is your aunt Connie well enough to take over? Except for Emma in preschool, the kids are in school full-time, so someone else could—"

"I'll give you until Christmas, Tessa. I want an answer before Christmas Eve."

"I'm not sure I can be here on Christmas."

"You'll be here. The kids are already making decorations and planning activities. They have Christmas all planned out."

Danny's high-handed attitude robbed Tessa of words. His next statement robbed her of the entire English language.

"You have to stop running from love sometime, sweetheart. I think a Christmas wedding is the place to do it."

IF TESSA THOUGHT she'd have peace and quiet to brood over Danny's ultimatum, she was mistaken. Not only was she swamped with holiday parties after she and Barrett had made such a splash with their winter wonderland party, but the kids had last-minute school plays and concerts. Then there were the traditional holiday visits. Since Danny's kids had asked her family to attend their events, too, she barely had time to think about Christmas, much less finish her shopping. As she and Rhonda wandered through a department store the Saturday before Christmas, Rhonda stopped so suddenly that Tessa ran into her and dropped her shopping bags directly in front of a bunch of kids racing through the aisle. Tessa rescued her bags from the marauding herd just in time.

"You, kids, stop running," Tessa yelled after them.

Rhonda started laughing. "That didn't sound like the quiet, repressed Tessa Doherty who moved here last spring."

"What do you mean?" Tessa asked, stuffing the last of her packages back into her bags.

"She would have been icily polite, careful not to make a scene in public."

"I wasn't making a scene. I was telling those kids to slow down."

"Yes, at the top of your lungs," Rhonda agreed.

"Why did you stop so fast, anyway?"

Rhonda grabbed Tessa's arm and twirled her around. "Look."

Tessa looked around. "Look at what?"

"That dress on the mannequin."

"What about it?"

"It's perfect."

"Perfect for what?"

"For your wedding, of course."

Tessa groaned. "Rhonda, not you, too. You're my best friend. You're supposed to be on my side."

"I am on your side. I'm almost pasted there. And because I'm on your side, I'm not going to let you make the biggest mistake of your life."

"I've already made that one, remember? I married Colin."

"Colin was a step on the path to where you're supposed to be, that's all."

Tessa sent her friend a suspicious look. "Are you still dating that new-age massage therapist? I thought you broke up."

"We did, but he won me back when he started talking about our auras intermingling. It sounded so sexy we ended up in a storage closet at the hospital."

Tessa laughed. "You're incorrigible. I'm surprised you weren't caught." At Rhonda's expression she laughed harder. "You were caught."

"Not caught, exactly, but we sure got some knowing looks when we emerged from the closet. I didn't know it until later, but my shirt was on inside out."

Gaining control, Tessa said, "Rhonda, this is so like you. Remember that time when—"

"Stop that. We're talking about your wedding dress here."

"No, you're talking about it. I'm trying to change the subject."

"You love him, don't you?" Rhonda demanded. "Don't tell me you don't, because you've been miserable not seeing much of him for the past two weeks. Your kids are complaining, Danny's kids are complaining, Danny's coworkers are complaining…."

"Yes, okay, I love him, but— How do you know Danny's coworkers?"

"I've been in touch with CJ Doren. She told me he's been like a tiger with a toothache at work."

"He has?"

"Yes, and you're just as bad."

"I am not."

Rhonda steered Tessa toward the mannequin. "Yes, you are. That's why we have appointments for facials, hairstyling, pedicures and nails later this afternoon."

"I can't do that. I don't have time. I have a million things to do."

"Make the time. You're starting to resemble an anemic ghost." Rhonda pointed at a full-length mirror. "Look at yourself."

Tessa peeked. "Oh, come on, I don't look that bad. It's the department-store lights."

"Trust me, you look that bad. The shadows under your eyes look as if a vampire bit you two days ago. And don't get me started on your hair."

Biting her lip, Tessa said, "I'm tired, all right? I haven't had time to primp. I work for a living, remember?"

"So do I, but I still wear some makeup and style my hair, not just yank it back into a ponytail. You're lucky you're so pretty, Tessa, or little children would run in terror."

Tessa held up her hand, palm out. "Stop. I get the point. We'll go to the salon."

"You bet we will. Right after we try on that dress."

'I don't know if—"

"Stop it, Tessa. You love him, he loves you. You'll work out the problems as you go forward. Do you want to end up a little old lady with nothing but regrets and cats? 'Cause that's the direction you're going."

"I'm scared, Rhonda."

"Who isn't? But Tessa, if you don't marry Danny you'll still be scared, but you'll be alone. Is that what you want?"

"No. No, I don't."

Rhonda dug her phone out of her massive tote bag and handed it over to Tessa. "Then call Danny and tell him so."

Tessa hesitated, then took the phone.

"Meanwhile, I'm going to take that dress to the dressing room for you. And don't worry about arranging the wedding. I already have everything under control. It's almost all finished."

Tessa almost dropped the phone. "You, you, you…what?"

"What are friends for? I knew you would say yes eventually."

"I, you…"

"Now, call Danny before I have to do that for you, too." Rhonda walked away chuckling as she heard the firm way Tessa was punching in Danny's number.

"HEY, SANTORI," Jake Doren called across the firehouse garage, "the chief wants you on the double."

Danny hung up his cell phone and shoved it into the holster at his waist. He pushed away from the fire engine he'd been inspecting when Tessa called. "Where is he?"

"In his office."

"Right." He punched Jake's arm, giving him a big smile. "Thanks."

"No problem," Jake replied, his attention already diverted by the arson canine investigator coming into the garage with his black Lab heeling at his side.

Danny strolled into Mike's office. His chief was standing by his desk talking on the phone. "Yep, I agree…right. I'll let you know how it turns out."

Mike waved him to a seat as he hung up the phone. "How's it going, Danny?"

"Good."

"Good," he repeated. "I was just wondering how you're doing lately."

Danny sent him a quizzical look. "What are you, my mother?"

Mike grinned. "I like to know what's going on with my department, that's all."

"You seeing some problems I don't know about?"

"Nope, nothing like that. I've been hearing that you're kind of touchy these days, but…"

Danny grinned. "Who's touchy? I'm fine. Nothing's wrong."

"In that case, am I invited to a wedding on Christmas Eve?"

Thrusting his hands into his pockets, Danny rocked back and forth like a proud little boy. "You sure as hell are. You're the best man."

"Everything is okay, then?"

"Sure is. Damn good thing, too, because the kids have been bugging the hell out of me with questions about decorating the house for a wedding, plus Christmas. That was just the start. Aunt Connie told me she's handling the catering and then she called my mom and aunt in Missouri asking them to come up. The pastor called me the other day to say he's booked and can't wait to perform the ceremony. I even got a call from Barrett, that florist guy Tessa works with, about the flowers. If Tessa hadn't finally said yes I wouldn't have been able to hold my head up again."

"Congratulations. Better you than me," Mike said with a grin.

"Your turn will come, pal. I won't be happy until the entire squad is married."

Mike laughed, then indicated that Danny take a chair. "Remember I told you I had something else in mind for your career? Well, this isn't official yet, but our assistant fire chief has resigned. He's moving to Texas. This means I need an assistant chief. How about it?"

"Me? You're offering it to me, you mean?"

Mike grinned. "Do you see anyone else in here? Yes, you. You've been here over twelve years. You've worked your way up to captain and know administration, how to handle people and firefighting procedures. I've already got the blessing of the bosses. What do you say?"

A bit overwhelmed, Danny couldn't answer for a moment.

"You'll have an official ceremony, but I wanted to tell the superintendent that you've accepted the position. This way your hours would be regular daytime ones. You'd be on call when needed for a run just as I am, but you can get a more scheduled life for your family by doing this."

"Mike, I don't know what to say."

"Say yes or no, Santori."

"Yes," Danny said, standing to meet Mike's handshake. "Thanks."

"Don't thank me. You earned it."

WEARING A NEW NAVY SUIT, white shirt and silk tie with Santas on it, courtesy of his children, Danny stood by the Christmas tree in the same living room where he'd once interviewed Miss Peach to babysit for his children. The room was a bit different now, decked with lighted candles, flowers, Christmas decorations and wedding bells. He looked around, scarcely seeing the smiling friends and family who were gathered there to watch him take the plunge.

"Don't try it, Danny," Mike Crezinski said with a bracing slap on his back. "The squad would tackle you before you got near the door."

"I'm not going anywhere."

Danny turned when the sounds of the wedding march began. As the music strummed he looked down the makeshift aisle that divided the small crowd. The first thing he saw was Rhonda surrounded by a loud group of excited children, slicked and scrubbed in their shiniest Sunday best, assembling at the back of the room. Rhonda, his mom and Aunt Connie were attempting to restore order.

"Quiet," Rhonda said. "Whisper."

"Kyle, Kevin, knock it off," he heard his mother say.

"I forgot my underpants, Alison," Emma said.

Alison groaned, but Aunt Connie had a solution. "Don't do any cartwheels, Emma."

"Okay."

Order was finally restored and Rhonda paced with the music toward the tree where the pastor, Danny and Mike waited. Alison followed looking very grown-up to his eyes. Danny focused his attention on the next group, hoping his younger children would make it to the front of the room without incident. He gasped, and then grinned as he saw something he'd missed before— General was part of the group. A leash of ribbons held by the twins was restraining the four-legged member of the family. General wore a dog-happy grin and stopped to bestow an occasional lick on the guests before continuing down the aisle.

"They're not bringing the squirrel, too, are they?" Mike whispered.

"Bite your tongue," Danny muttered, chuckles from the room recapturing his attention. Down the aisle came Josie with a solemn expression and Emma with her little mouth stretched in a wide smile. Emma was waving at everyone and Josie was tugging at her own ribbon leash. No squirrel followed them, though. Instead Fuzzface, the black kitten Danny had rescued and given to Tessa's children, was rolling along behind, playing with the ribbons. Finally Josie had to stop and pick him up as she and Emma hurried the rest of the way to the tree. Little ham that she was, Emma curtsied to the chuckling crowd while Josie started to something to Danny. Thank heavens the guitar player began singing at that moment.

All eyes went to the back of the room.

At the sight of Tessa, all Danny's nerves fled. All he could think of was how beautiful she was in the ivory lace dress that hugged her figure. She wore no veil, just a few simple flowers in her hair that matched the casual bouquet of roses and ivy accented with red and green bows and sprays of white and silver. She looked nervous, but still so lovely she took Danny's breath away. Tessa started down the aisle, her arm entwined with Eric's, who was a bit pale but smiling as he manfully led his mother toward Danny.

When Tessa's gaze met his, the love in his heart overwhelmed him. Her hand reached out to meet his waiting one. As they touched, he had a vision of their life together. He couldn't wait for it to begin.

It began as soon as the pastor pronounced them man and wife, and he kissed her for what felt like the first time.

Raising his head, Danny whispered, "I love you, Tessa. I promise to show you how much later."

After another kiss Tessa whispered back, "I'll hold you to that promise. I love you, too, Danny."

Their loving moment was interrupted by a swarm of children and friends circling them with hugs, kisses and congratulations. The guitar player wailed an energetic celebration song at the top of his lungs, with a barking dog and the meows of a frantic kitten accompanying it all. Life was back to normal. The only thing they could do was go with the flow as the champagne corks popped, the beer tabs snapped and the food was devoured.

FINALLY GUESTS WERE GONE, kids were tucked into bed to dream of Santa Claus and his presents under the tree, and the house was quiet for the night. Now Tessa and Danny could pick up where they had left off at the altar.

"About that promise," Tessa reminded her husband as she

dropped her silk negligee on the floor beside the bed. She climbed onto the mattress where Danny already waited, with only a sheet covering his eagerness to get his hands on his wife.

"What promise?" he teased.

"Well, if you need reminding," Tessa said as she slipped the silk nightgown off her shoulders, laughing as Danny tumbled her onto the sheets.

"Oh, that promise."

His lips met hers and conversation ceased as their hands avidly explored each other's bodies, relearning each curve and angle, experimenting with touch, with taste, discovering thrills of emotion pulsing with anticipation.

"Have I told you how beautiful you are?" Danny murmured as his lips caressed her skin, kissing and licking his way down her curves to her sweet spot.

Tessa groaned as her body responded. "Tell me again."

"I'll tell you later," Danny said, caught in his own response as her fingers wrapped around him.

The only sounds now were soft moans and whispers of delight as he entered her and brought them both to the peak until they finally flew over into satisfied contentment. Close in each other's arms they slept until a pounding on the door wakened them. They surfaced from a long and satisfying night to the early-morning sounds of excited children.

"Santa was here. Santa was here," the twins' voices echoed.

"There are so many presents under the tree!" Josie squealed.

"Come on, you guys, get up. We want to open the presents." The twins were getting impatient.

A small fist pounding on the door followed the twins' knocks. "He ate all the cookies, Daddy!" Emma yelled.

"Shut up," Alison said softly. "You'll wake them."

"They have to get up—it's Christmas," the twins yelled at their sister.

"Get downstairs right now," Eric ordered, followed by what sounded like a herd of elephants pounding down the steps.

Still entwined and cozy in their bed, Danny laughed. "Good thing we locked the door, huh?" He rose on his elbow, dropping a kiss on Tessa's lips. "Well, Mrs. Santori, ready to face the mob?"

Tessa giggled. "If we don't, they might break the door down next time." She watched as Danny got up, yanked on a pair of flannel pajama bottoms and grabbed a sweatshirt with a grinning snowman's face on the front. "Danny, did I tell you how happy I am?"

Danny grinned. "I got the idea last night."

"I was so scared. Then I saw you by the tree and it all clicked. You were the man I wanted. I wondered why I'd been so afraid to take the step, why I kept trying to push you away…."

Danny laughed. "But I wouldn't go."

"No, you wouldn't. Thank heavens for your stubborn streak, Danny Santori."

"I like to think of it as persistence and determination in the face of obstacles. You, my darling wife, were the biggest obstacle I'd ever come up against."

Grinning, Tessa tossed a pillow at him, which he ducked to avoid before yanking the covers off Tessa. "Get out of that bed, woman, or I'll have to get back in. Then you'll be sorry."

Tessa stretched, her pose as provocative and inviting as she knew how. "Sorry? Really?"

"Don't tempt me, sweetheart. Remember that speech you gave me about responsibility. Right now you and I are responsible for six kids not knocking over the Christmas tree to get to the presents." Danny yanked her out of bed and placed a light swat on her naked behind. "You have two minutes to cover that luscious body or I'm not responsible for the consequences."

After another tempting grin back at him, Tessa threw on

her own Christmas sweatshirt with a grinning reindeer, and matching pants.

As they made their way down the stairs the sounds of excited kids swelled from the living room. When they walked into the chaos the kids were already stretched under the tree hauling out the presents.

"Say when, Dad," Kevin or Kyle said. Tessa decided she'd have to color someone's hair so she could tell the two imps apart, since their cuts had grown out.

Tessa elbowed Danny. "What does he mean?"

"The past few years I've yelled 'go' and let the kids start unwrapping. What do you do?"

"We take turns so no one misses anything." She glanced at the excited children poised over their gifts. "You know what? I think I like your tradition better." She melted at the look of love in Danny's eyes.

"You sure?"

"Absolutely."

Danny stood up. "Okay, kids, everyone have their own presents? No cheating. On my mark, ready, set, go."

Ripped paper floated to the floor, ribbons flew and squeals filled the room. Not to be left out of the action, General and Fuzzface dashed into the mix with lots of growls, meows and chasing around the excited children. Tessa curled next to Danny on the sofa and watched, calling comments as she saw the gifts.

She looked over at Alison, who'd gone very quiet as she stared into a box she'd just unwrapped. "My own phone? Dad, you gave me my own cell phone?"

Danny smiled. "Tessa convinced me that every girl needs a phone in her room so she can share secrets with her friends. Don't take it to class—leave it in your locker."

"Mom, look, I got all this new software and games."

"It goes with the new family computer in the den," Tessa

said. "Danny told me a house with six kids needs more than one computer or we'd never be able to use it, too."

"Sweet," Eric yelled. "Can I go…?"

"Not yet," Danny said. "After we open some more gifts."

Josie and Emma showed their princess dress-ups, Barbie dolls and play kitchen set, and the twins their new racetrack and monster games. When the voices died down, Danny stood up and asked the kids to get the two gifts for Tessa hidden behind the tree.

Tessa pointed. "Wait a minute, there's two back there for Danny also. Bring those out, please."

"You first, Danny," Tessa said. He started to refuse and insist she go first, but she shoved the first gift into his hands. "This is from me and the children." He tore into the wrapping as enthusiastically as his kids and pulled out a soft leather briefcase.

"I thought the new assistant fire chief might need one."

"It's terrific—so soft." His hand caressing the leather brought back erotic memories to Tessa, so she thrust the other gift into his hands to take her attention off her libido.

"This is from me."

Danny unwrapped the box and gave a shout of laughter as he pulled out a T-shirt that said This Fireman Belongs to Tessa and She Belongs to Him. He leaned over to kiss her. "So you're giving in, going to be an obedient little wife?"

Tessa arched her brow. "Aren't you the one who's always saying I didn't mean it the way it came out?"

"Now you, Tessa," Alison urged, stopping the teasing conversation. "Open yours."

Danny handed Tessa a small box. Tessa detached the bow, then opened the paper with careful movements.

"Honey, it's only paper. More is available."

"Hush, I'm saving it for a memory box." She folded the paper and put it aside before opening the gift to reveal… "A key?"

"That's right, a key to your very own office and work space."

"What are you talking about?"

"I rented it for you."

"You what? Where…how…?"

"I was talking to Barrett. You know that Victorian mansion he's renovating for his business?"

"Yes. It has a greenhouse on the property, too, doesn't it?"

"That's the one. He has quite a bit of leftover space for another office and workroom. He was thinking of renting it, but wanted to find a business that complemented his, and of course the right person. I suggested you and he jumped at the deal. Barrett said he wouldn't hold you to it if you don't like it. But I figured a businesswoman needs her own location."

For a moment Tessa had no words. Deciding she didn't need any, she jumped into Danny's lap and covered his face with kisses, accompanied by the appropriate giggles, horrified ooohh, gross and kissy sounds from the kids.

"I guess you like it, huh?" Danny said when he could breathe.

"Open ours next," Emma and Josie urged.

Danny handed over the second present. "This is from all of the kids."

"Don't open it like an old lady this time," one of the twins urged.

Tessa laughed and ripped the paper, flinging it into the mess on the floor. "How's that?" She flipped open a box and gasped. "Oh, oh, oh, this is too much."

With reverent hands she lifted the door plaque from the tissue paper.

"I can't believe it," she said as she read "Living Lifestyles, Tessa Santori, President." She started to cry.

Not sure what to do, the kids tried to comfort her. "No, no, I love it, " she reassured them. "I'm just…I can't believe it's happening, that's all."

Again the children's chorus chimed in.

"Girls."

"Silly Mommy."

"Tessa's a crybaby."

"Shut up, Kevin."

"Knock it off, you guys."

"That's enough. Everyone in the kitchen," Alison ordered. "We're making breakfast, remember?"

The kids trailed out of the room, leaving Tessa and Danny alone.

Danny folded her in his arms and leaned back on the sofa. "Well, Mrs. Santori. When you're a successful mogul, I expect you to keep me in luxury."

"You can be my houseboy, how about that?"

"Do I have to do dishes?"

With a suggestive wink, Tessa said, "I'm sure there are other things you can do with your time."

Danny traced her lips with his finger. "You'll find me up for the chore."

"I'm sure I will," Tessa murmured, caressing his face as he kissed her.

"Merry Christmas, Tessa. I love you."

"Merry Christmas to you, darling. I love you, too." They became lost in their own little world for a few moments.

"Hey, you guys, look," Kyle yelled from the kitchen. "They're kissing again."

"Gross," Kevin said, following his comment by blowing raspberries. "Are they going to do that all the time?"

Danny chuckled as he suited action to words. "Damn right we are."

* * * * *

Celebrate 60 years of pure reading pleasure
with Harlequin®!
Just in time for the holidays,
Silhouette Special Edition® is proud to present
New York Times bestselling author
Kathleen Eagle's
ONE COWBOY, ONE CHRISTMAS

Rodeo rider Zach Beaudry was a travelin' man—until he broke down in middle-of-nowhere South Dakota during a deep freeze. That's when an angel came to his rescue....

"Don't die on me. Come on, Zel. You know how much I love you, girl. You're all I've got. Don't do this to me here. Not *now*."

But Zelda had quit on him, and Zach Beaudry had no one to blame but himself. He'd taken his sweet time hitting the road, and then miscalculated a shortcut. For all he knew he was a hundred miles from gas. But even if they were sitting next to a pump, the ten dollars he had in his pocket wouldn't get him out of South Dakota, which was not where he wanted to be right now. Not even his beloved pickup truck, Zelda, could get him much of anywhere on fumes. He was sitting out in the cold in the middle of nowhere. And getting colder.

He shifted the pickup into Neutral and pulled hard on the steering wheel, using the downhill slope to get her off the blacktop and into the roadside grass, where she shuddered to a standstill. He stroked the padded dash. "You'll be safe here."

But Zach would not. It was getting dark, and it was already too damn cold for his cowboy ass. Zach's battered body was a barometer, and he was feeling South Dakota, big time. He'd have given his right arm to be climbing into a hotel hot tub instead of a brutal blast of north wind. The right was his free arm anyway. Damn thing had lost altitude, touched some part of the bull and caused him a scoreless ride last time out.

It wasn't scoring him a ride this night, either. A carload of teenagers whizzed by, topping off the insult by laying on the horn as they passed him. It was at least twenty minutes before another vehicle came along. He stepped out and waved both arms this time, damn near getting himself killed. Whatever happened to *do unto others?* In places like this, decent people didn't leave each other stranded in the cold.

His face was feeling stiff, and he figured he'd better start walking before his toes went numb. He struck out for a distant yard light, the only sign of human habitation in sight. He couldn't tell how distant, but he knew he'd be hurting by the time he got there, and he was counting on some kindly old man to be answering the door. No shame among the lame.

It wasn't like Zach was fresh off the operating table—it had been a few months since his last round of repairs—but he hadn't given himself enough time. He'd lopped a couple of weeks off the near end of the doc's estimated recovery time, rigged up a brace, done some heavy-duty taping and climbed onto another bull. Hung in there for five seconds—four seconds past feeling the pop in his hip and three seconds short of the buzzer.

He could still feel the pain shooting down his leg with every step. Only this time he had to pick the damn thing up, swing it forward and drop it down again on his own.

Pride be damned, he just hoped *somebody* would be answering the door at the end of the road. The light in the front window was a good sign.

The four steps to the covered porch might as well have been four hundred, and he was looking to climb them with a lead weight chained to his left leg. His eyes were just as screwed up as his hip. Big black spots danced around with tiny red flashers, and he couldn't tell what was real and what wasn't. He stumbled over some shrubbery, steadied himself on the porch railing and peered between vertical slats.

There in the front window stood a spruce tree with a silver star affixed to the top. Zach was pretty sure the red sparks were all in his head, but the white lights twinkling by the hundreds throughout the huge tree, those were real. He wasn't too sure about the woman hanging the shiny balls. Most of her hair was caught up on her head and fastened in a curly clump, but the light captured by the escaped bits crowned her with a golden halo. Her face was a soft shadow, her body a willowy silhouette beneath a long white gown. If this was where the mind ran off to when cold started shutting down the rest of the body, then Zach's final worldly thought was, *This ain't such a bad way to go.*

If she would just turn to the window, he could die looking into the eyes of a Christmas angel.

* * * * *

Could this woman from Zach's past
get the lonesome cowboy to come in
from the cold...for good?
Look for
ONE COWBOY, ONE CHRISTMAS
by Kathleen Eagle
Available December 2009
from Silhouette Special Edition®

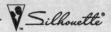
™ *Silhouette*®

SPECIAL EDITION

**FROM *NEW YORK TIMES* AND *USA TODAY*
BESTSELLING AUTHOR**

KATHLEEN EAGLE

ONE COWBOY,
One Christmas

When bull rider Zach Beaudry appeared
out of thin air on Ann Drexler's ranch,
she thought she was seeing a ghost of
Christmas past. And though Zach had
no memory of their night of passion years
ago, they were about to share a future
he would never forget.

*Available December 2009
wherever books are sold.*

SSE65493

Visit Silhouette Books at www.eHarlequin.com

REQUEST YOUR FREE BOOKS!
2 FREE NOVELS PLUS 2 FREE GIFTS!

HARLEQUIN®
American ★ Romance®

Love, Home & Happiness!

YES! Please send me 2 FREE Harlequin® American Romance® novels and my 2 FREE gifts (gifts are worth about $10). After receiving them, if I don't wish to receive any more books, I can return the shipping statement marked "cancel." If I don't cancel, I will receive 4 brand-new novels every month and be billed just $4.24 per book in the U.S. or $4.99 per book in Canada.* That's a savings of close to 15% off the cover price! It's quite a bargain! Shipping and handling is just 50¢ per book. I understand that accepting the 2 free books and gifts places me under no obligation to buy anything. I can always return a shipment and cancel at any time. Even if I never buy another book from Harlequin, the two free books and gifts are mine to keep forever.

154 HDN E4DS   354 HDN E4D4

Name	(PLEASE PRINT)	
Address		Apt. #
City	State/Prov.	Zip/Postal Code

Signature (if under 18, a parent or guardian must sign)

Mail to the **Harlequin Reader Service:**
IN U.S.A.: P.O. Box 1867, Buffalo, NY 14240-1867
IN CANADA: P.O. Box 609, Fort Erie, Ontario L2A 5X3

Not valid to current subscribers of Harlequin® American Romance® books.

Want to try two free books from another line?
Call 1-800-873-8635 or visit www.morefreebooks.com.

* Terms and prices subject to change without notice. Prices do not include applicable taxes. N.Y. residents add applicable sales tax. Canadian residents will be charged applicable provincial taxes and GST. Offer not valid in Quebec. This offer is limited to one order per household. All orders subject to approval. Credit or debit balances in a customer's account(s) may be offset by any other outstanding balance owed by or to the customer. Please allow 4 to 6 weeks for delivery. Offer available while quantities last.

Your Privacy: Harlequin is committed to protecting your privacy. Our Privacy Policy is available online at www.eHarlequin.com or upon request from the Reader Service. From time to time we make our lists of customers available to reputable third parties who may have a product or service of interest to you. If you would prefer we not share your name and address, please check here. ☐

HAR09R2

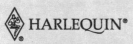

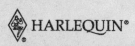
HARLEQUIN®

American ★ Romance®

COMING NEXT MONTH
Available December 8, 2009

#1285 THE WRANGLER by Pamela Britton
Men Made in America
For as long as she can remember, Samantha Davies has dreamed of Montana's legendary Baer Mountain mustangs. She has to see for herself if there's truth behind the legend...before she loses her sight forever. And nothing, not even the devil-handsome wrangler Clint McAlister—who has every reason to distrust Samantha's intentions—is going to stand in her way. Because time is running out.

#1286 A MOMMY FOR CHRISTMAS by Cathy Gillen Thacker
The Lone Star Dads Club
With four preschoolers between them, neighbors and single parents Travis Carson and Holly Baxter don't know what they'd do without each other. And they don't want to find out! Everything changes when Travis's little girls ask Santa for a mommy for Christmas. Their entire Texas town gets in on the hunt for an available mom...who happens to live right next door.

#1287 HER CHRISTMAS WISH by Cindi Myers
The only thing Alina Allinova wants for Christmas is to stay in the U.S.—oh, and Eric Sepulveda. They're having a fairy-tale romance, yet the possibility of sharing a happily-ever-after seems far away, with her visa expiring soon. Still, her fingers are crossed that come Christmas morning she'll get her wish and find him under her tree!

#1288 A COWBOY CHRISTMAS by Marin Thomas
2 stories in 1!
The holidays are a rough time for widower Logan Taylor and single dad Fletcher McFadden—neither hunky cowboy has been lucky in love. But Christmas *is* the season of miracles! Logan meets his match in "A Christmas Baby," while Fletcher gets a second chance at love in "Marry Me, Cowboy." This year both cowboys are on Santa's Nice list!